I0762352

PRAISE FOR NORA LANGE'S US FOOLS

- National Book Critics Circle Award for Fiction—*Finalist*
- Sue Kaufman Prize for First Fiction from the American Academy of Arts and Letters—*Winner*
- *Los Angeles Times* Bestseller
- A Best Book of the Year—NPR, *The Boston Globe*
- Editors' Choice Pick—*New York Times*

"Great American Novels are still being published in 2024 and here is one of them." **—MOLLY YOUNG, *NEW YORK TIMES***

"This novel is tender and exceptionally moving, but also mordantly funny in parts, and it's a razor-sharp critique of American capitalism. And it's written so beautifully that it's hard to believe it's a debut novel." **—MICHAEL SCHAUB, NPR**

"Exquisitely funny… a novel that is uniquely and urgently about and for today, mapping the uncrossable distance between the coasts and the heartland, between the America we've been and the America we want to be. Its reward is to witness a rapturous and rare kind of truth. This savage American novel consumed me, as much as I consumed it."
—ELEANOR HENDERSON, *NEW YORK TIMES*

"Lange's style is complex and comedic… it is quite remarkable."
—JANE SMILEY, *LOS ANGELES TIMES*

"Lange's achingly stylish prose, brutal humor, and ferocious wit set this novel apart—she captures the tender and complex ways that growing up and growing older can impact sisterhood."
—KIMBERLY KING PARSONS, *LITHUB*

"Lange writes in dense paragraphs full of harsh wisdom—vodka tossed on scraped knees—with the ideas and intensity of six novels in one. The result is a fully American artwork that shames, decimates, invents, and reinvents. And reinvents, and reinvents."
—RYAN CHAPMAN, *BOMB*

"Lange's debut novel is a refreshingly sardonic take on the decaying ideal of the American dream, with an anti-capitalist tilt. At the end of it all, this is not just a brilliant bildungsroman: Like the classics that the Fareown sisters quote ad infinitum, it's a lush, uncanny mythology itself." **—*KIRKUS REVIEWS*, STARRED REVIEW**

"You could read Us Fools as a tight-knit family drama, an historical look at the farm crisis, or an exploration of how economic realities can force us to pick an identity. But more simply, Lange says, it's just about America." **—ANDREW LIMBONG, NPR**

Day Care

NORA LANGE

Two Dollar Radio

Books too loud to Ignore

WHO WE ARE Two Dollar Radio is dedicated to reaffirming the cultural and artistic spirit of the publishing industry. We aim to do this by presenting bold works of literary merit, each book, individually and collectively, providing a sonic progression that we believe to be too loud to ignore.

An imprint of SEVEN STORIES PRESS.

Proudly based in **Ohio**
TURTLE ISLAND

TwoDollarRadio.com

@TwoDollarRadio

/TwoDollarRadio

Printed in Canada.

ISBN 9781953387578 *Library of Congress Control Number available upon request.*

Also available as an Ebook.
E-ISBN 9781953387585

Book Club & Reader Guide of questions and topics for discussion is available at twodollarradio.com

SOME RECOMMENDED LOCATIONS FOR READING:
Pretty much anywhere because books are portable and the perfect technology!

AUTHOR PHOTO Helki Frantzen.

COVER PHOTO Photo by sareh Askarzadeh on Unsplash.
COVER DESIGN Eric Obenauf.

Stories have appeared in slightly different form in the following places: "Hotspots," *The New Yorker*; "Day Care," *Granta*; "Heart Beats," *BOMB*; "The Craftsman," *Denver Quarterly*; "Fork," *Juked*; "Owls Yawn Too," *LIT*; "Encounter Beach," *Birkensnake*; "Last Boob Feed," *Hazlitt*; "Throwback," *Hobart*; "Dog Star," *The Rupture*; "Letting Snails Go," *Joyland*; "Her Cousin Lena," *American Short Fiction*; "Distrito Federal," *Hobart*; "Panel vs. Board," *Two Serious Ladies*.

Two Dollar Radio would like to acknowledge that the land where we live and work is the contemporary territory of multiple Indigenous Nations.

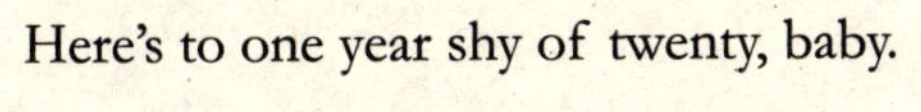

Here's to one year shy of twenty, baby.

Day Care

Table of Contents

Heart Beats

Carol and David were last to arrive for the dinner party. The looks they received from the other guests, already drinking martinis on the rickety porch, were not subtle.

"What's a dinner party without a bit of schadenfreude?" Carol whispered into David's ear, her lips pricked by the coarse hairs that grew there like weeds.

Carol made light of being late, but she was still embarrassed. She blamed David for not taking the empty parking space she'd pointed out to him. As they drove in circles, David insisted there would be an even better spot closer to the party at Sharon and Ray's.

But there wasn't, and when they drove back around, that space was no longer empty. Carol would address this and other matters later with David, after getting stoned, when the stakes of addressing matters were significantly muddled, when her hair was down and detangled, her legs lathered in soothing lotion, and their kids were fast asleep.

"Look around," David said of the perky Boston neighborhood, handing Carol a dry martini. "Note all the people going about their everyday lives."

"Have you ever noticed the closer a monkey looks like a man, the sadder the monkey looks?" Carol asked. David was not amused.

The neighborhood was anticipating a final balmy summer night. American flags waved on lawns, barbeques were blowing up, and children were falling off skateboards. The police were out in force, which was often the case when the weather was good and the rules went out the window. A bunch of cops loitered around Spokes, the rowdy and popular biker bar on the corner. The last time Carol went to Sharon and Ray's for dinner she came alone and parked near Spokes. She stuck her head inside the bar just to see what the fuss was about. A tall, handsome man wearing black leather chaps and a blue bandana offered to buy her a shot, any juice Carol desired, and she found herself wondering if her hosts had a first aid kit in their austere home.

Sharon and Ray hosted dinners regularly.

Carol didn't know Ray well, but there was a lot she admired about Sharon, her gritty co-worker at the County Supervisor's office. Sharon was Sharon on her own terms. And grit was an asset in this world where getting by seemed to be getting harder and more strained. Several years ago, Sharon had returned to Boston, the place of her birth, to care for her mother. This detail struck Carol; Carol would never return to where she grew up. The place didn't bear naming. Also, Carol's mother was insane. Her mother's inquisitive mind long lost to the domestic, too often misconstrued as the home. Her enfeebled body was the result of cleaning houses, running errands, and caring for other children belonging to wealthy families. Carol's mother went through her entire life without anyone stopping to ask her what she wanted.

"It's time to party," Sharon said, motioning for their guests to take their seats around the table.

Sharon and Ray's Victorian was a fixer. Sharon said she thought the old house was a complete and total failure in judgment, a fucking marriage disaster, both structurally and psychologically. It was like they didn't know what to do with the place. Stacks of books, magazines, bills, clothing, and piles of their baby's "water colorings" snaked throughout. Carol was in awe of the disorder; she ran a tight ship. She was rarely tardy. She kept their house spotless. Carol disliked piles. She was not a pile person. She disliked leftovers. Carol's mother made food in order to have leftovers. She kept track of when supermarkets offered samples, and when she saw the samples, she stuffed her pockets and purses sideways. The food decomposed on countertops, even spoiled in the fridge. Vermin took over the one-bedroom apartment until Carol showed up to get rid of the detritus.

At the table, Sharon and Ray's one-year-old spoke her first word. The baby pronounced "ass" with exceptional clarity. It could not be confused. Sharon shot Ray the "hold down the fort" look and excused herself, taking their baby out of the room. Carol knew that look well. She'd shot David that same look across many tables, in many rooms, many times over the years. Carol could draw that look in the dark.

"My nephew's first word was 'why,'" one guest said to the table. "Can you imagine?"

Carol knew Sharon's husband edited paparazzi videos for a living. In his line of work, obscenities were ordinary. Their baby might have heard something. On numerous occasions, Sharon showed Ray's work to Carol: videos of underage starlets waving, playfully flashing their faultless titties, but then without warning the starlets might scream and spit cucumber ginger elixirs onto intruding photographers. Sharon said that for years Ray talked himself out of blame for the ethical lines that were crossed. Ray wasn't the one snapping the photos! Or taking the footage! He was just a loner editing the material in a stuffy office space. And since their move back to Boston, Sharon had said to Carol, Ray was just himself, a political centrist with a protruding gut.

The scene at the table was lackluster.

Sharon was the light of the party and was off putting the baby to bed. This left a vacuum for others to indulge in, or develop, bad habits like complaining about how late it was getting and distracting themselves with handheld devices. David texted Carol, *It seems everyone might as well go home and give themselves enemas*. One guest, who'd introduced himself as a financial advisor, started talking about how he'd once led a cult in Arizona called The Banshees. Apparently, they licked dirt and rubbed their bodies on cactuses.

"We were seeking to mimic the behaviors of Indigenous Amazonians. We drank hallucinogenic concoctions to cleanse our bodies, to rid our bodies of toxins, and in great ecstasy we shat and vomited all over each other," he said.

David texted Carol, *Wow, this guy's a real nutjob.*

The cult leader turned financial advisor should have known better than to establish a cult camp in the desert where there were limited resources. Carol was certain that this guy, a white guy from Massachusetts, never had and never would live like an Indigenous anybody.

Carol texted David, *Let's hope this guy doesn't have a gun. I'm starved.*

Ray got up to open windows. Guests mingled. Carol was ready for Sharon to return and pull out the good weed she kept tucked away in her underpants. Sharon's go-to strain was called Girl Scout Cookies. She preferred that strain to others because she'd once been a Girl Scout, a terrible one. Sharon had been slow to learn new skills. She couldn't sell the popular cookies. She was fat. She barely fit into her slender Girl Scout uniform. Her skin showed through the gape of her shirt front. The other girls never let her forget. Carol admired that about Sharon, the way Sharon subverted her torment, rolled it and smoked it; she published a guide on surviving aspirationalism, and when celebrity crotch shots became a thing, she wore military surplus briefs. Sharon drifted toward the underworld but never sank.

It started to pour. Ray went to get some rags to put down beneath the open windows. Another guest piped up to tell the group that he wasn't much of a baseball fan. He just never got into baseball.

"It's not like I don't go to games," he recklessly went on, ignoring Boston's general mandate to avoid subjects like baseball. Fights broke out over allegiances to players, umpire calls, and curses.

"I do. I go to Red Sox games like any other loyal Massachusetts resident, but unlike other Bostonians I'm just not that into the crowd. Plus, the beer's not all that great. It's sort of watery and flat-out expensive."

Carol watched as the cult leader turned financial advisor seethed, adjusting his Red Sox baseball cap and rolling up his shirtsleeves. His jaw clenched. His chest puffed up. He had the look of a man about to punch another man. Sort of thrilling.

David was about to text Carol when Carol texted David, *Stop texting me, David.*

"Settle down and be a sport," said the wife of the cult leader turned financial advisor. To which he said, "I am a fucking goddamn sport. You of all people know that."

Sharon and Ray had marital arrangements. Sharon had said as much to Carol over work breaks. One such arrangement included a swapping and owning of time. 2017 was slated to be Sharon's year. A solid year would be hers to do with what she liked. She might take a road trip, leave the baby with Ray and his videos, go someplace in the middle of the country, someplace she knew nothing about. Sharon spoke about time like time was simply a matter of when one would get it back, like buying a round of cocktails for friends at a bar. Sharon conceded that compartmentalizing time into "your year" and "my year" was a stalling tactic. Time wasn't static, Sharon knew that, but the arrangement provided a way forward in her marriage. If she accepted that the day of repayment would never come, she might as well vanish, and that was too much to ask of anyone.

"Let's go ahead with dinner," Ray said.

The rain smacked the roof. Carol wondered if David had closed the car windows, and even though he sat next to her, she was too lazy to text him or ask. The car was parked six blocks away. Parking was such a scene in Boston that at one point Carol and David considered moving out of the city to Braintree. But after Carol read a line in a small poetry book breaking down the words, where a brain gets snagged in a tree, she never read poetry again and gave up the idea of moving out of the city.

Sharon came back to the table just as Ray was serving the dumplings and herb salad. Sharon passed around crumpled cloth napkins and settled into her chair. She lit a joint.

"There's a theory," Sharon said, "that all species have the same number of heart beats. The difference between how long they live depends on how fast or slow their heart beats. Hummingbirds have short lives and whales have long lives." A saucy dumpling landed on Sharon's thin pale-green blouse. She didn't notice.

David had sex dreams about Sharon. He'd told Carol about them. What could be wrong with fantasizing if it presented a way around the limitations they'd set? He dreamed of sex with Sharon on pristine Hawaiian beaches. Another variation involved having sex while snorkeling. And then there was the occasional jumping out of helicopters. When Carol dreamed, she dreamed of her childhood bedroom, which was not sexy. The bedroom was full of boxes and ghosts. The same ghosts every time.

The light above the table flickered. It was an Ikea bulb. Nobody kept Ikea replacements around. The cult leader turned financial advisor asked the table if they had ever lived without electricity.

"In the cult we lived in teepee-like structures in the Arizona desert. We didn't have electricity. No internet, hairdryer, or Vitamix," he said. "We were out there in the Arizona desert, shitting in plastic buckets."

Carol offered to serve Sharon's mother's famous peach dessert and left for the kitchen. The kitchen counter was stacked high with dirty dishes, smudged glassware, and empty bottles, indicators of an evening going well. Carol also spotted nipple shields, dying aloe plants, and half-checked grocery lists. Items checked: calm tea, sleepy tea, sponge?, sammich stuff. Toilet paper and frozen waffles were also accounted for. The two items left unchecked were a log of goat cheese and onions.

Carol returned to the table with dessert.

The guests were in the same arrangement, like they were waiting for a director. The room was growing darker, outside stormier; the plates before the guests were empty. It was like a Brechtian play, bare and estranged. The best kind of theater. Carol snatched the next joint from Sharon's fingers and smoked on it, hard. She spooled out the gooey peach crumble and found herself in a Western. She was Clint Eastwood. She was a Western. Lawless and in open skies. Peach goo attached to her fingers. She would leave it there to dry out. Save it for later. Jesus, that sounded like her mother.

Settling back into her seat, stoned and comfortable, Carol wondered what David looked like copulating underwater with Sharon. How did that fantasy work with the snorkeling gear, David? Carol understood irony and social protocol. When their kids were tucked in bed, she'd masturbate to the BBC like Regan gave her body to Satan in *The Exorcist*. In England, manners and conversational protocol were indistinguishable, a constant. So much betraying in reasonable voices made Carol envious of the synchronicity, of having it both ways. In America, socializing was called mingling, or hanging out or flirting, depending on the company. It was messy.

A guest who'd remained quiet up until that point suggested they play a game.

"A kinky sort of game, if you're up for it," she said.

The men twisted in their chairs. Their sense of self was being put on the spot. They were often blamed for spoiling the mood, and here they were again presented with another challenge. If they said no, what would become of them? If they agreed, what would become of them? The uncertain, concerned looks on their faces, like Catholic schoolboys waiting to be scolded by the headmaster. The women were amused, excited by prospects involving the unknown.

"I'm down," Sharon said, leading the way.

2017 was Sharon's year.

Carol too was curious. She was also curious about this woman, who'd said nothing until then. What had made her speak up now? Carol looked down at her palm. She thought about the dirty twenty-five-year-old she let touch her at Costco. A few days ago, she'd gone there for alone time. Instead, she met a kid that reeked of kerosene, standing in front of a row of flat-screen TVs. He said news was bad for the brain and with his dry hands started touching her face. She didn't stop him. The touching continued: eyelids, throat, collarbone. Her stomach turned. She lost track of where his hands were and of the time. He was nothing like her. He believed 9/11 was a government conspiracy and tried showing Carol videos to prove it, but YouTube had started limiting borderline content. Just his luck, he'd lamented, writing his phone number with a permanent marker on the palm of her hand. Carol went for her cell, it wasn't there. Where was her phone? She didn't know or care. She was at Sharon's, high on Girl Scout Cookies, and savoring every thought-kernel like a burst of sour lemon. Looking at Sharon's blouse, Carol made a joke about the greasy splotch left by the fallen dumpling.

Sharon said she wasn't going to bother trying to get the stain out, not by washing it now, or soaking it later, or by using her "anytime instant remover" Tide stain stick. In fact, Sharon wasn't going to get up from her chair unless it was a life-or-death situation, and even then, she wasn't sure.

Everyone devoured the peach crumble. The quiet woman explained she'd overheard people talking about the game on public transit. She hadn't seen the people, but she'd heard them say it was liberating. She wrote the name down in her notebook, where she kept her observations. David also kept a pad of paper. He listed the instances when Carol was right and when he was wrong and stored it on his side of the bed.

"We need a volunteer to download a questionable app on their phone," the woman said.

The cult leader turned financial advisor handed over his Blackberry.

"For the team."

The game worked like spin the bottle, except that the stakes were more extreme. The rules would become more obvious once they got going. And the group would be using a cellphone instead of a bottle.

Sharon snatched the joint back from Carol. It was a nub. She pulled out tweezers to smoke on it and called Carol a bitch.

"If we're doing this, let's do it. It's time," Ray said, opening a bottle of beer with a lighter and dropping the cap to the floor.

Carol looked at David, and David looked at his watch. Her phone had fallen under her chair. She picked it up and texted David, *There's plenty of time.* They had six hours before tomorrow's alarm would go off, unless their kids got them up beforehand. But even then, they were accommodating children. Their children knew when times were tense. They did more around the house: taking the trash out, watering the plants, cleaning their rooms, staying out of the way. They did all this without being asked. But they were still children and children shouldn't be expected to be adults. Carol and David were the adults.

Earlier at the park their seven-year-old had fallen, slicing her knee open on a rock. Carol and David had expected their daughter to sob when she noticed her bloody knee; when she didn't sob, they definitely thought she would sob when she noticed how distraught they were at the sight of her in pain. Instead, she took one look at her bloody knee, then at Carol's and David's faces, and went back to playing.

Can we start this evening over? David texted Carol.

"Begin," Sharon said, blowing smoke out of her nose like a snail leaves a slimy trail.

Sharon spun the Blackberry with a quick twist of her wrist. It didn't circle as a bottle of Mickey's had back in the day, but it whirled around, stopping in front of David. Carol noticed that David shot up from the table like he did when his legs went numb and tingly on airplanes. In a block of forest green, the phone blinked *Fuck*. It was like a siren. The table was alert, like finally, after years of waiting patiently, the authorities had given the adults permission to pee in the community pool.

"On second thought," Sharon said, sliding a saltine into her mouth. "It's my year and my party and I'm spinning again."

The phone spun and landed on Carol. Again, the forest green *Fuck*. Carol gently folded her napkin before standing up. Sharon launched her soiled napkin across the room. Charmed creatures, the two of them left the table, and while whispering, closed the bedroom door, taking the air out of the room with them. Who would run the show?

David helped himself to a finger of gin before pouring one out for Ray, one for the cult leader turned financial advisor, and one for the baseball hater. The men were second-guessing the game idea but collectively knew they couldn't and wouldn't back out. They drank.

The cult leader turned financial advisor pointed to Ray, "Come on. Your turn, man. Do you need someone to sing you a song?"

Ray needed something. It wasn't a saltine or a glass of water. He gave the Blackberry a spin. He was determined to play by the rules, not to be a pussy. He was fucking co-hosting this dinner party too, though it wasn't technically his year it was one he was living regardless. The phone landed on the cult leader turned financial advisor. It flashed *Choke* in bright orange block letters.

"Let me offer an explanation," said the woman whose idea the game was in the first place. "You get choked until you cum. It's relatively straightforward. You can read more about the technique on dangerandplay.com. The site is full of a bunch of crap, but it does provide some useful instructions."

David was about to text Carol, *You're missing the real show now.*

"It could have been much worse," said the woman. "You could have been stuck with *Bind, Blind, and Tease*, which would have been a lot more involved."

The cult leader turned financial advisor's wife asked about *Bind, Blind, and Tease*, but took one look at her husband, who she was sure might have a modicum of interest in this sexual awakening. He had recently left his porn out, she presumed for her to find. His face was not one of delight. He was seething and turning whiter with rage. He told Ray to meet him in his black Audi SUV, parked outside in front of the fire hydrant, impossible to miss. It was black with tinted windows and custom detailing. He got up from his chair and left.

As much as Ray would have liked to fasten his hooks around that guy's neck, Ray didn't need to see him jackoff. But he wasn't about to play the role of the downer. Ray readied himself. He opened another window, letting in more of the night's air, which brought with it the smells and scents of others. Sharon liked when the air circulated, the more frigid the better. She preferred the air when it pierced. Ray drank the last of his gin and realized he'd need some props, or at least a hand towel. He avoided making eye contact as he left the table. In the bathroom, he took from the cupboard a freshly folded cotton towel depicting glittery unicorns and green elves atop mountains and castles. He smothered his face in the fabric.

The remaining guests were relieved to see Ray reemerge and then exit the house. It was someone else's turn to spin, but without their hosts around to enforce cooperation they felt liberated, like children covering their eyes with cupped hands.

"What did Jesus say? Carpe diem?" David said, his voice breaking. He instantaneously felt foolish he hadn't listened more to Carol about self-editing. The cult leader turned financial advisor wouldn't have been so easy to read.

"Nah," said the guest who knew about sex games. "I need to dash."

"I'm going to call a Lyft," the wife of the cult leader turned financial advisor said. "I'm wiped and I have early barre tomorrow."

"That shit's tough," baseball-hater agreed. He said he was tired and prone to migraines, the aura kind, flashing lights and so forth. Nothing helped. Plus, he was trying to lose weight, trying to get his heart rate up, winter was around the corner and they wouldn't see light for days on end.

David texted Carol for the sake of texting Carol, *The guests are fleeing, even nutjob guy is gone. You can come out now. I'm here.*

Carol's cell vibrated on her empty chair.

David picked up her phone and unlocked it. It was easy, their first child's birth year and two of Carol's favorite numbers back-to-back. From her phone, he texted: *I love you, David. Now, go fuck yourself.*

Last Boob Feed

I imagine eggs, imagine whipping the yolks in a glass bowl with a fork and lightly scrambling them. But by the time I open the refrigerator my appetite has evaporated. Nick is buttering an everything bagel. He is topping it with everything-bagel seasoning. I picture my mother. The '80s version of her: rail-thin like a scarecrow, her breast milk dried up, cutting out coupons to stack in a neat pile, chain-smoking Benson and Hedges Ultra-Light Menthols, doing taxes—endless—in the kitchen with flowery linoleum flooring that she'd wipe clean on her knees. My mother bruised easily.

Today, I will consume my mother. That's what you do when you've lost someone. And to do this consuming of my mother, I will purchase a funnel. That's how you slow down the process of absorption when, unsolicited, your in-laws come to visit to be helpful and tell you you're too skinny. Do you feed this baby? they ask. Soon your body will disappear like condensation dribbles down a shower door into nothing, they don't say. For days afterward, this baby screams at the boobs. The internet says she is protesting. Nick says to please close the refrigerator door, otherwise the food will rot.

I have this baby. We have this baby. This baby emerged like a lightning bolt onto the scene—this was how I preferred to see the hospital room, surrounded by strangers, and where the lower half of my body knelt bare, a leftover part like a tree stump in the woods. Those present at her birth said that watching her be born was like nothing they'd ever seen. But I cannot imagine this to be true. She's been here this whole time. This baby is of the forest. We, you and I, were painted back into the image. You and I are the ones who are fortunate to be allowed to join her in her environment, and if we're not careful, we could just as easily be taken away. Not she, or the clouds and trees, I say, or so I think. Only much later do I realize I did not speak for days after giving birth. I have misplaced my voice like a set of house keys and people keep saying, *No worries, those things are not lost, they've just gone missing*, and I want to seismic-volcano shit on their faces like this baby does in her sleep. When this baby shits like a volcano she is calm, and she is this enviable way because she is telling the truth.

Nick and I bring this baby home to find that the crows have left feathers by our front door; the squirrels have left acorns—some intact, others cracked—there too. Those first few weeks, ladybugs managed to enter, without ingress, to fly around our bedroom in the attic.

In public, strangers tell me many things about this baby. Perfect strangers have a lot of thoughts, even when they're passing by hastily. I wonder if they're so thoughtful on their own time, alone, no human in sight, in their bedrooms, coming to grips with what ails them. Nobody once mentions to me that babies are ravenous. This baby came starved. But by the time I'm willing to share this about hunger, everyone has vanished. The stage has been emptied; the cast and crew have gone, leaving plastic water bottles and sandwich crusts strewn throughout the parking lot.

Nick tells me about this wildly popular woman online who says cribs are cages. Babies need to be free to sleep where they want to sleep. Apparently, she's a personality. I haven't read this myself, but Nick, father of this baby, finds it amusing. Our senses of humor have diverged these past three months. He knows everything there is to know about keeping this baby safe. He listens on triple speed to the best baby audiobooks for beginner parents. I'm not losing my hair along with this baby, he says, as is to be expected. I write myself an email reminder to boob-feed the baby. Nick continues. He says I am a goddess, empties another box of red wine that he keeps chilled in the fridge, and spins the hairs on his chest like he's screwing in little screws until they have become ingrown and inflamed.

It takes some doing, some mustering of internal resources, but I try to get out of the house daily to see the sky or the ruptured sewage pipe. Most of the time, once outside in public, I get distracted by the drone that someone uses to monitor the landscape. It zips by, buzzing. When this baby is napping, in the privacy of the bathroom, I will unearth my folded sheets of paper from beneath a packet of baby wipes made almost exclusively of water, and I will continue drafting my war plan to devour it. The drone, of course.

When the day feels unending, I try to get to the sidewalk and make sure to look, really look, making use of the things we do not ordinarily use to observe—using my jaw and skin, the largest organ in our body—at the toppled traffic cone, lying on its side on the mud in front of the meth-house where they've been digging up the sewage pipe. To prepare for this, I put on what I have handy, which is a gray synthetic nursing sweatshirt, and head for the front door. Nick follows me closely. He asks what I'm up to. Off to see the sky, I tell him, ruefully. He would prefer me to stay inside and write, or at least write hate-mail to the designers of this nursing sweatshirt. He doesn't even think the sweatshirt is worth donating. The drawstrings were poking the baby's eyes while she was fiend-feeding. He had to find scissors that worked to chop them off so that they wouldn't poke this baby's eyes out. This search of his—to locate working sharp scissors—took time.

From the sidewalk, I find my tongue, which has been on holiday, and roll the word *fuckwad* around in my mouth like a marble, immediately feel unkind, and immediately feel exhausted. I have again forgotten to brush my teeth. I wish dental floss were called *crevice pleaser.* I wish there were more inventive ways to fool ourselves. How much will I need to relinquish to not fail this baby? Or do I mean this body?

I look down to be sure I'm still covering my breasts, which, like garments dangling on a backyard clothesline, do their own thing in the wind without my knowledge. And then there are the origins of things. Ceres, the mother of agriculture in Ovid's myth, scours

Earth for her abducted daughter Proserpina, who only hours earlier had been dancing in a field of flowers. Jupiter, super king of gods and Proserpina's father, will urge Ceres to compromise. He will encourage Ceres to view the child's abductor as not so bad—these things are nuanced, he'll be candid. Moreover, super god Jupiter reasons: If this daughter does not belong in hell, then she will not be tempted to eat the food in hell. Even I know hell's food is the only food. This daughter will eat hell food. Her tortured existence, her nature divided—seesawing between heaven and hell—will give us the seasons. Like one of those constant tickles at the back of the throat, a persistent voice has another message: If only I could be so lucky. Like my mother, I say deranged things and wish to be as free as I wish to be.

I begin to clean the dirty railing with the sleeve of my synthetic sweatshirt, which works wonders, and I am annoyed it has taken me so long to figure this out. Nick leans over the railing with this baby draped over his shoulder, says it's pretty chilly and asks if I'm warm enough.

My mother's middle name became her first name. She gave it to me as a middle name, which has stayed my middle name, and most call me by both my first and middle, swizzled together. I have named this baby after my mother's mother, my grandmother, who died when my mother was in her twenties and therefore was dead by the time I was born. This baby will never meet her grandmother either. My mother, living, refuses to see me. I have done something willfully tragic. I only eat hell food. I have asked for a break from my stepfather. Because of this, my mother explains via email, if she were to see me, she would be betraying him. She elucidates: Therefore, she refuses to meet this baby. Like I know nothing of explicitness.

Every time I pause to draft a response, to write my mother that this baby is just a baby and knows more about betrayal, along with all the other babies, than anyone, my boobs start burning.

The sky cracks, streams of light pour over the busted sewage pipe, and then the sky dumps rain. This phenomenon, water dumping from above and the city flooding, is known as an atmospheric river. A man from the meth house has come outside to move the mud around the fractured sewage pipe with a shovel, but he does not right the fallen construction cone.

I need a few things from a big store. A huge well-lit store. I leave Nick with this baby and take myself to Home Depot to buy a funnel and an imperfect square of laminate flooring that I will put on my pillow to later rest my head. Deva, a tall brunette with flashy red clogs, which click and clack, asks how many yards I'd like. What do I need? I am close to the part of Deva's chest where her name tag hangs. Her exposed mouth smells of sugary cinnamon gum. Deva, who smells of warm, inviting spices, is asking me what I need in yardage, and the lighting in the aisle is unflattering and her shoes are her transportation.

I drive home from Home Depot chewing five sticks of gum, thinking about origins, wads, and delirium. My desire to drive toward oncoming traffic is a result of delirium. Listening to the news, this is what I tell myself about delirium. The windshield wipers make a wretched weeping sound as they struggle to mitigate the downpour. This baby has started to cry out in her sleep. A terror howl, a wild, shrill beast pitch only another beast would know. I refuse to name and therefore understand the sound. I cannot handle the meaning, especially while driving. Or, as my mother would say: I cannot go there.

There's a woman standing in the median, a stroller stuffed with plastic bags full of her belongings. Cars drive past in a hurry to run the red light. I stop at the red light and feel out of touch. I worry the neighbors we share the duplex with will complain about this baby to the ruthless management company, who will find a way to evict us. Property values. I fear those we share our walls with will turn Nick and Me and This Baby in for being alive in the winter. This blurry accusation is unfounded. I know very well that I am delirious. Furthermore, our neighbors are liberal. Their values are expressed on their delineated part of the property. Their signs are written in both English and Spanish. One such warm sign says WELCOME in Hebrew. It hangs in their window with the dark curtains drawn. I pass, trying to catch a peek inside their half of the duplex like a pervert. I would like to know how they've handled the layout. Wearing my gray titty hoodie, I think—fascism is in vogue.

Back inside our part of the duplex, I don't feel like being a good mother. Parched, I go looking for my mug in the shape of a walrus. The one mug I've carried with me from job to job, apartment to apartment, across America, and I cannot find it. Nick says I'm smacking my gum; he doesn't think he's ever seen me chew chewing gum before. He wonders if I'm OK. Is it called chewing gum so you don't do something foolish? I do not ask. I've misplaced my walrus mug of decaf for the seventh time in four days. I won't do the math. Nick says to make a new one—to give myself a fresh cup of freeze-dried instant decaf from Europe. Maybe, I think, and wonder how Nick knows it's from Europe since I've covered over the label with a glossy sticker depicting two dolphins catching air. It wasn't that expensive, Nick says about the coffee. This would be a great opportunity to show him how much I love him, but I am relentless. I've spent twenty minutes ignoring him, staring at a hairy black spider on the ceiling that is harmless. The bath Nick has made for me has turned cold. He doesn't need to say it. The spider is very still. I say BOO—and nothing.

"Re: last boob feed" is the subject of an email thread I started from myself to myself after this baby was born; she'd lost so much weight after coming home from the hospital that I began keeping a diligent record of her feeding. I no longer mark whether it's a.m. or p.m. It's a collection of times that run together, which can read like an abstract painting reads. Several nights ago, it seemed this baby was officially done with me and the boobs: too much environmental stress and exhaustion. I began to cry, thinking it might be the last time I hit reply to the last boob feed email. There are so few connections I am reluctant to relinquish them.

Our bedroom is in the attic. Every night the three of us crawl up there to attempt sleep. This baby sleeps next to us in her own little bed. If she doesn't, we are told we will kill her. That is not what we want most of the time. To be safe, she will sleep there next to us in her bassinet for the next several months until she is able to sleep alone. I wonder if I'll toss out the baby monitor. But I wish to be another kind of mother. I am determined to be different, until I realize we're all addicts. Addicted to our pain, to cable, to whatever.

Nick sleeps naked beside me. I am wearing the heavy blankets around my neck like I've been beheaded. The father of this baby is smiling in his sleep. I am relieved he has found some joy with his eyes closed and I feel joy next to his joy. The room is alarmingly quiet. I check on this baby. Though this baby lies still as the dead, she is breathing. I feel her. Again, I pull the warm blankets back up around my neck, only to discover the wad of gum from earlier has gathered my hair into an orb of a mess. Anne Boleyn did not need her head to remain impactful—truth. The weather in Great Britain isn't all that different than it is here—also true. Also true—Anne Boleyn had a baby who became the greatest queen there ever was.

I remind myself this baby does not belong to me. She has been here all along. She is of the forest like trees are of the forest. Her presence comes from every direction like a compass. I am a guest in my life. Where did I put the funnel? I wonder.

Before bed, I bathe this baby in the bath, as my mother did with me, though in the shower, singing songs like "You Are My Sunshine," as the words were written inside a waterproof songbook, like time stood still, which it very well might in water. In the bath, I sing songs to this baby, ridiculous songs that I make up on the spot, and she behaves as though she is singing along. This evening, in the bath, she didn't allow me to remove the dried milk solids encrusted around her mouth in the shape of another mouth. Though she remembered the trick the hospital midwife taught us: my mouth kisses on her mouth so that she will open her mouth to latch.

It's too dark now to see it, but in our bedroom there's a large ornate mirror that hangs on the wall, which is beige. The entire room is painted beige, a true beige. The large mirror was a gift from a friend in Mexico. What I like most about it is the reflection. In the light, from where I lie, mother of this baby with no mother with no mother, it reflects the opposite wall, also beige, such that it doesn't seem like a mirror at all.

Island of Phaetons

“Why do you stand there lurking as all men lurk?” she asked, mostly jokingly, the friend that had wanted more than friendship, standing in the doorway to her apartment. It was her last night in Istanbul before traveling to Greece to meet up with Mary Beth, her adoptive mother who carried news with her from America. Rebecca was sitting cross-legged on her living room floor, surrounded by sheets of newspaper and painting supplies. She wore pristine white denim shorts that hit just above her knee. Her hair, dark, was in two tight braids. Her scalp was visible. On her laptop, a British police procedural was playing.

“It’s not really about solving problems, is it?” she asked the friend, who had a spare key to her apartment and was as close to her as anyone had been in a year. It seemed to Rebecca that those characters on television, as in life, had found a self-satisfying, near-sadistic interest in missing the point. And this, for her, had bludgeoned any chance of experiencing pleasure. She had a habit of downloading these homicidal dramas illegally and spending her evenings consuming them, waiting for the detectives to see the whole picture.

“Ovid had lost children,” she said of the crying, displaced boy on her screen, wandering alone in a forest, looking for someone to care for him.

Rebecca, an American academic teaching in Istanbul with her husband, had been taking her students on day trips to Büyükada, the largest of nine islands that made up Istanbul’s Princes’ Islands in the Sea of Marmara. Once there, students would forgo their smartphones to hike up to the monastery, or to visit the surviving remains of the orphanage. On the island, they would ride in horse-drawn carriages and over packed lunches discuss why a father had made an untenable promise to his boy, Phaethon. In Ovid's myth, exhausted by shame, the boy begs his mother, single and mortal, which students agreed was a compromising position, to prove that his father is who she claims he is—the Sun God. Moved by her son's anguish or piqued to refute the incessant rumors of her madness, she arranges a meeting between them. On meeting, Phaethon begs his father to remove all doubt about his legitimacy, henceforth removing the uncertainty which plagues him. To erase all fear, the Sun God promises to grant the boy anything he wishes. The boy—young, misguided, perhaps greedy for more—demands his father's chariot and the reins to steer his wing-footed horses for a day. As a result, the boy burns. And with his pulsating, incinerating body he takes much of Earth down with him. At the orphanage, nibbling on fruits, the students would discuss whether the boy was better off for knowing his father. Some were adamant that he was not. Others were unsure—as perhaps it was worth being legitimized.

"Samples." Rebecca indicated over her shoulder to varieties of blue paint, paintbrushes, and a piece of burlap on the floor next to her, covered in tiger-striped hues of the color. Rebecca told the friend—a German man who wanted more than friendship, who lived in the building and who worked at the same university up the Bosphorus—to enter the apartment to drink to her precarious visit to see Mary Beth. They'd better get started, she told the friend. Tomorrow would be long, and they should get on with hearing each other out. Her flight to Athens was ungodly early. And from there, she'd need to take an assortment of buses until boarding her ferry to the island of Hydra to join up with her mother and get caught up on "the latest." There was no doubt in Rebecca's mind that the news would be epic. Her mother had a peculiar way of landing herself in unsettling situations, usually revolving around notions of fate, which of late had meant synchronizing oddities in sets of three and usually involved terror and a man. Mary Beth loved chess, but she could never be counted on to finish a game. Mary Beth loved starting things, like motherhood, but she had a difficult time seeing things through. She would predictably have with her a bottle of lube, a picture of Matt Damon from 1998 from an unknown source, and a slim diary she had begun the year she adopted Rebecca that she'd hoped to one day fill.

"Maybe don't ask," Rebecca said, opening a bottle of red Assyrian communion wine, a varietal called Boğazkere, which she understood meant "throat clencher."

She cracked a kitchen window. The evening August air rolled in. It was summer in Istanbul. Teenagers were sitting on steep staircases, smoking, and drinking bottles of Efes. Middle-aged men were sitting in parks, rolling prayer beads between their fingers. Yellow taxicabs were competing for customers. From Rebecca's window, you could spot the dozens of healthy stray cats maneuvering the retaining walls—towering vertical concrete slabs with tiny purple and orange wildflowers bursting from the cracks.

Rebecca had an indent in the back of her head the size of a hamster, the result of being dropped as a baby, and not as a joke: "Did you know this about me, that I would have another hamster in a heartbeat?" she asked. "These quiet good-natured pets don't live long."

He assumed there was an embedded joke in that.

Mary Beth, who insisted on being called both names, which Rebecca punctuated like popping apricot pits out of her mouth, had said the dent was a blessing. A sign of good things to come. An omen. Her mother, eventually settling on being a speech pathologist after years of outlining possibilities—entrepreneur, medical researcher, CEO, venture capitalist, marketing brand manager, business consultant, investigative reporter, military strategist—had left Rebecca a message saying she'd updates, but she wouldn't say *what* until Rebecca was in Greece with her. The possibilities, endless, left Rebecca with little choice but to oblige—she could not leave her mother if her mother had asked for her. What kind of daughter would that make her? Rebecca had thought that moving far away to a country like Turkey, a place everyone she knew back home believed was in the Middle East, might have allowed for her to go quietly.

That night before Rebecca's trip to Greece, she and the friend who wanted more than friendship stood in her kitchen, drinking. Rebecca spoke of this knife, the size of a man's sternum, that her stepfather, Mary Beth's fourth husband, wore around his neck. Her stepfather had explained that there were cougars running amok in Carlsbad, California, where she'd spent her elementary school years, when really her stepfather was a beastly man with a ferocious temper. In her kitchen in Istanbul, Rebecca clawed at her neck and went from talking about her stepfather, to wine aging in clay amphora, to Easter: "A ridiculous day that involves the resurrection of Jesus, pastel-colored eggs, and humans sweating profusely beneath synthetic bunny costumes."

But that wasn't exactly what she had in mind to talk about that night before her flight. As it turned out, months earlier, while a group of her colleagues from the university brunched in her apartment to acknowledge Jesus' resurrection gesturally, Rebecca had been in the bathroom. Her back had been propped up against the moist toilet. She was looking down at the stunning Ottoman tiles covered in her blood. She'd miscarried. And all she could think about when she looked at the remains was which products would clean those stunning ancient tiles thoroughly. She didn't like leaving messes, ever. Those months ago, she had found herself contemplating self-preservation and mythmaking—whether the two were linked, dependent on one another, or were they antithetical?

Rebecca set her glass of wine down on the kitchen counter. She put a dollop of kaymak on a brownie. She then shoved the clotted cream-covered brownie into the German friend's mouth as they heard the door to the apartment slam. It was Rebecca's husband. He entered the kitchen, which immediately turned suffocatingly moist. He was amped—his veins were showing through his skin. He went to touch Rebecca. First, her cheek using the back of his hand, miming a playful threat, then lightly tapping her shoulder with his fingertips, and finally her ass with his palms.

"Wish me happy birthday, Rebecca," he said in a drunk, delicate voice.

"It's not your birthday, Ian," she responded, reflexively.

Rebecca excused herself. She explained to the two men standing in the kitchen that she had to finish painting the ceiling a resonant sky blue before her morning flight to meet Mary Beth. If she, Rebecca, were lucky, she might be able to differentiate herself from her mother—i.e., not follow the same sorts of paths. Her story had the ceiling a crystal blue.

The next day the friend that had wanted more than a friendship went by the couple's apartment to wish her a safe trip. Rebecca's husband, barefoot and shirtless, greeted him at the door. He wore loose boxers, the flesh of his genitals visible. The husband wielded a kind of certainty; the friend observed.

"Being an American must be magnificent," he said about him to him.

It seemed to allow the husband to move through the world like he owned it. The husband said he did. He explained to the friend that he did own it.

"You just missed her," the husband added, widening the apartment door to Vanna White the ceiling that had been completed. Rebecca had finished painting it and she was already in a cab on her way to Atatürk Airport.

Rebecca was on board her flight that had been delayed. She was stuck on the tarmac for the unforeseeable future. She was getting cozy, consuming a British drama on her cellphone. She remained buckled in, even though the plane, due to unforeseen technical issues, would remain at the airport until those issues were resolved, which could take a lifetime. Rebecca had helped herself to a second small bottle of gin from the flight attendant, who had become her buddy.

"What's in Greece?" asked the flight attendant, who was from

Greece and lived in Greece.

"The Cradle of Western Civilization," she said flippantly and because it was true. Rebecca said that she was going to see her mother, which caused the flight attendant to turn her lips inward as if she were in pain.

Eventually the man who was seated next to Rebecca left. The flight attendant, who'd been hovering to chat with Rebecca, went ahead and took his aisle seat. It was as if the arrangement had been preordained.

She and Rebecca agreed that television had really taken a dip. It had lost any sense of poetry. Each had a partner who felt painfully misunderstood. Rebecca's had kept her up into the early morning hours, discussing his PhD, and how nobody seemed to understand his value. Nobody except for Rebecca. The flight attendant nodded in approval. She said she hoped for their sakes that their spouses would find peace. She said that sometimes a person just needs to force quit.

"We designed the machines, after all," she said of partnerships and electronic devices.

The other flight attendants were serving the other patrons onboard, and as they performed this service it seemed to the two new buddies that all anyone ever did was demand something more. They talked about getting away.

"Even children at two years of age knew to ask for space. I masturbate in the bathroom before the smell in there becomes unbearable," the flight attendant said.

Rebecca was surprised to hear the nasty smell was possible even on short flights, such as from Turkey to Greece. The best thing about her job, the flight attendant said, was moving through the atmosphere.

Had the flight attendant heard the news about this woman who was said to have disappeared? There had been a recent segment on the radio, a story about a woman that had been billed as a tragedy. Rebecca wasn't so sure. The woman had been a professional, a wife, and recent mother of twins, who one day up and left, never to be heard from again. Her family, close friends, co-workers, nobody knew where she had gone. And this woman was the kind of woman who made friends with everybody, the radio announcers made sure to point out, which was to say she had no enemies. She made others happy. Yet, poof—she'd vaporized. No voicemail. No explanation note next to the çaydanlık keeping the tea hot. All she'd left was a large pot of soup on the stove, which Rebecca and the flight attendant noted was very thoughtful.

A week passed. Another week went by before the friend ran into the husband outside of their apartment building. The husband seemed well, if a little disheveled. He was dressed in a nicely ironed shirt that he had buttoned incorrectly. His teeth seemed straighter. His skin, rougher. Both men were returning from a trip to the market for the basics—eggs, bubble bath, rakı. The husband explained that he was going to try to catch some nightlife at a hip new club up the coast later and asked the friend of Rebecca's if he would join him. The friend demurred—he'd a backlog of student papers to grade. The two stood there lingering in the foyer, taking turns admitting that they missed her.

Had the friend seen the ceiling? He had. The husband had shown it to him himself, remember? Together, loitering at the entrance to the building, they came to a joint consensus: the painted blue ceiling in the apartment was striking. So alarmingly oceanic that when the two men slept, they dreamed in the very same iridescent shade. There was no escaping it.

Rebecca had sent the friend a worn, beat-up postcard from Hydra. Or he thought it was from that island. The husband had received one of those in the mail, too. Or so he believed. Neither one could make out the image or the text on the cover. The ink was blotchy. The content indecipherable. They stood there fiddling with themselves, waiting for the other to say something useful, before realizing that they had no clue where they'd put the damn things. Both reasoned that they must have stored the postcards someplace remarkable. Hidden the mail in one of those special, elusive, secret spots you trust you will find again when you go searching for it. The sorts that will reveal themselves when you least expect it.

Hotspot

The younger sister, one of two siblings, sat at her desk with a view of the park and counted swollen pigeons. She should have been applying for jobs. But the sister no longer had high-speed internet. The brother had stopped paying for it—he had to draw the line somewhere. He had no intention of bailing her out again, and he said as much to her over the phone. The sister had made a habit of sketching babies and watching pigeons eat trash in a park rather than uploading her resume. However, he would continue to pay her phone bill. For months, the steady older brother in Hoboken with resources had paid her rent and now he scolded her during their weekly check-in call. The sister resisted mentioning that he *would* bail her out. The brother worshiped the feeling. He would succumb to this need to be needed. She may have been creative, job-less, and living in a dingy beloved studio in faraway Brooklyn, but she understood him. Theirs was the sort of familiarity that could pass only between siblings, each competing to survive.

"Quiet," she hushed the brother. The pigeons had cleverly discovered something underneath a stroller and were making efforts to dislodge it from the wheels. From her perch, it appeared to her to be lasagna. Those long thick noodles were unmistakable. The brother talked as the pigeons nibbled away, and a new desire-rash began forming on the sister's left knee. The latest, more of an auburn, complemented the earlier pink splotch that now covered her other knee.

"You're exhausting," he said to her during their weekly check-in call. He was right. She had observed that wearing people out, stripping them of their energies which allowed them to think clearly, was how successful people such as the brother managed to pilfer all the resources.

The brother had been the one to suggest that the sister use her phone as a hotspot. He liked knowing something about technology. It made him feel in-touch, like back when he went clubbing with the cool kids hellbent on dying young because that was the point. She thought the point was to be an artist.

"Last week I was on hold for seventy-nine minutes, trying to get through to Visa's fraud department, before giving up entirely," she said to her brother, who had his assistant perform these soul-sucking tasks.

The brother held an important position in a multinational company he had a hard time explaining the purpose of. He lived an undisturbed life in a New Jersey palace with his expectant wife and their four children, organized like cubicles. He suffered from unhappiness. He worked countless hours. His body was failing him. That Christmas, the sister noticed his hair and penis enhancement medicines in the cabinet when she'd gone to the far bathroom, seeking privacy and connection by way of ketamine and the internet. How else had anyone made anything of themselves? he'd said of her discovery. The brother and the sister stayed up all night laughing. The sort that had snot coming out of their noses. The type that had them aching.

The sister hung up on him. It was fine, the brother liked it. From her desk, her laptop took a bite out of her view of the park. Dozens of tabs were open, indications of potential, small and plentiful. Outside, there was a lady with a stroller moving quickly in the cold. The sister looked for clues in the woman's body language, something adoring and sympathetic, but could not decipher whether she was the child's mother. The sister was not going to have children. She was already in debt. Children—the ultimate signifier of wealth—had mouths she'd never be able to feed. Unemployment had her burying her preconceived notions about what qualified as a life. For roughly one-hundred and fifteen days she ate cold noodles, searched online for opportunities, and took bathroom breaks to flirt on her phone with an editor of a prestigious magazine he'd been hired to rescue, and did. Online was not really a suitable place to assess the merit of these exchanges, it wasn't even a place—she knew that. But the editor had said the magazine's craft essays *paid*. And he'd had her in mind to write one.

I'm your brother, he texted.

There was another woman with an infant, walking in the park. This time the baby was attached to the woman's chest. A new desire-rash quickly formed on the sister's thigh. Another atop it. The doubling burned a reminder; barking dogs you'd forgotten to feed. She put her hand on the pink splotch. It grew wider. The brother sent a follow-up text—the sister should focus on elder care. She clicked with older people. Plus, the generations were aging more rapidly than ever. The elderly were outliving the young—surely there were bountiful steady positions in this sector.

He called. She answered. He was her only sibling. He'd paid to have someone deliver her citrus so that she could avoid scurvy. She was in no position to lose his financial support. Kafka had died in a dark hole, like, a real shithole.

Into her ear, he rolled out the words *health business sector*, like he was ordering a dirty chai, as though he knew what it was. The sister told him she was hard at work on an essay about the landfill that as children they'd pass. Flirting with the editor did not interfere with her productivity. Besides, it was unlawful to prevent people from using the restroom, or from using their free time to pursue the subtext of life, which she would not say for fear of ridicule. (It should be noted that she had given up entirely on any need to be loved. She hoped the editor would like her essays and pay her handsomely for them.)

A friend, who'd kept a spare key to her apartment, entered and said, "What is going on here? Succulents could live through the world's end." The sister's plants were shriveling.

"Have you noticed that small breasts are out of fashion?" The sister's breasts were tinier than ever.

"It's time to leave," the friend said. Leave the craft-writing, slash, the job search.

The friend put a coat and scarf by the door. "Meet me at the place down the street for happy hour, dull as that may be," the friend said.

A slim flame of hope that would burn out completely when they got to the bar. Not only did the establishment no longer offer discounts on booze, but the free popcorn was now three dollars, mere chump change. In the past, that kind of cash—the right kind—would have gotten you a crisp beer and a soulmate.

At the bar, the sister drank club soda with a lime that she'd brought from her stash of citrus.

"Do you have high-speed internet? Do you have babies in your park?" she asked the friend, who lived in another borough.

The friend said she wasn't sure about babies in her park and left. She came back with tequila shots, immediately asked how much the magazine paid for craft essays, and admitted that it could be a set-up. The friend said she knew a private detective who owed her a favor. Then she noticed the sister's colorful rashes, which had begun inching up from beneath the collar of her shirt.

"Your arms are pink," the friend said, asking what was going on.

"Desire," the sister explained of her tattoo-sleeves made up of lovely rashes. "The spots just formed themselves."

"It's kind of miraculous," the friend said.

Back in the sister's studio, it had grown dark. The park lights had come on. The brother was calling. The siblings had already had their check-in call.

"I'm downstairs."

"It's a walk-up. I'm at the top."

"Of course you are."

It would take him several minutes to get to her. He didn't like to break a sweat. She closed her computer. She changed into a sundress to show off her colorful rashes, spots that just formed themselves; kind of miraculous when you thought about it.

The brother entered her apartment. He was never out of breath.

He was one of those people who could appear to be anything if it resembled perfection. He said nothing about her sundress and asked for food. That's what happened when one came to expect certain things—you convinced yourself that what you wanted to see was in fact what you saw. The sister noticed the black duffle bags limp on either side of his legs, little buzzkills.

He continued rifling through her fridge. She handed him stale popcorn and offered him nutritional yeast. He ordered delivery, asap. She prepared a grapefruit. They split it. The sister insisted he call his wife—she was going to have a baby soon. The brother insisted she tell him about the essay she was writing about the landfill of their youth. He demanded that she say more about working for the editor. She better write and make something of herself. The sister thought of something Patricia Lockwood had written: Some people can do cartwheels and other people do that thing where they put down their hands and then kind of hop off the ground. First, before any explanations, the brother needed a rinse. He welcomed himself to a towel and was intrigued to learn that he'd have to go down the hall to accomplish this. What might be in store for him along the way? The sister really did love him. His intention was to be helpful. But feared she would never be able to wrangle free from the debilitating cycle of debt that existed between them.

A desire rash crept in between the sister's lips. When she let it, her entire person would become a single, compliant hotspot on her very own terms. From the brother's phone, she texted the brother's wife, pleading for forgiveness: *Let me come home, let me back inside the palace*. The brother returned freshly rinsed, and the sister was nowhere to be found. There, in her absence, was a pulsating, hot-to-the-touch shape that continued expanding before him. He was simply beside himself.

Throwback

Last night I was visited by a spirit I made out to be my friend Naomi, who in 2016 wisely fled to Canada. In loose form, Naomi said: I've been reading your mind. You've been sick trying to figure out what happened to irony. With a snap of her fingers it's 2015, she and I are back in LA, walking our dogs in the summer heat. Spirit Naomi says we're all set to attend a wedding expo, *Lovesick*, which defined itself as having a taste for the unconventional, an alternative to all the regular bride bullshit out there. I'm not cut out to be a wife. I know that now, I tell her. She says, it promises to be ridiculous.

I've made bad decisions before, like LSD was worth a trip into the woods with a man who'd said he lost his identity in an end-of-world battle. Perusing the internet has become my porn, my Nora Roberts novel, which I refuse to surrender. I say this, and Naomi, in spirit form, shakes her head, disapprovingly. I remind her, that really, she's in Canada. It's 2020. All bets are off. If Anthony Weiner can repeatedly snap selfies fiddling with his penis that no one asked for, I'm not going down for feeling self-conscious about buying trash bags and slingshots from Amazon. The spirit tells me it's me, my news, that's outdated. OK. I feel a little self-conscious, but only because in the past I've made better bad decisions.

I show Naomi a panorama of 1993. Junior High: I'm riding skateboards, hanging out with gutter punks from Montreal (Canada too, I say), my tongue is pierced, safety pins puncture the skin around my bellybutton, I stalk people and negotiate trades, like weed, cigarettes, lip-gloss (whatever I'd stolen), for taking their photograph. I pretend to be older, mostly getting away with it.

The spirit is having none of my vision. Instead, she's guiding me to a bright Saturday afternoon in Los Angeles, to an alternative wedding expo. My husband-to-be smiles wryly as we depart: "Have fun." He means it as much as he can. He knows how I feel about comments that even imply the use of exclamation points. I study him like I'm seeing him for the very first time. For a second, I remember life before being evicted, the miscarriage in our bathroom on election night, and before my insomnia, up all hours, devising a break from our marriage.

Naomi says it's time to go. We park and walk over to the sign-in table where overjoyed greeters hand us our free tote bag. "It's gonna be fun! It's a tote bag!" I am terrified—too much expression is being expressed. Why am I here? I ask the spirit. Because, she says, you pitched *Jezebel* on a "Fear and Loathing at the Bridal Expo" piece. Don't worry, she explains, your editor will leave, and the incoming editor won't respond to any of your follow-up emails. I stuff the tote into my backpack. Within the expo's rented space there is another space called The Unique Space, which in 1996 we would have called *meta*. Naomi slaps me and tells me to pay attention. This alternative wedding expo has photographers, caterers, event planners, and dressmakers, even slow-motion video, skee-ball (one of the first redemption games), photo booths, a cocktail bar. Anything unique. Despite Naomi's objections, I go to the bar.

The bartender, a Jamie Dornan-type, says his company infuses their vodkas. "Yeah," the Dornan-type adds at the end of his sentence, landing like a wrapper, hopeless and in earnest like he is about to unlock the Red Room of Pain. I send Naomi a text: *Does he know what he sounds like?* She takes my phone away. Despite all the unwise decisions I've made, I found myself stuck between *B"rye"D & Groom*, a mix of green apple infused rye, butterscotch tincture, key-lime juice, lime, and sour patch candy. Or *Rose Lips*, a rose-infused vodka, muddled blackberry, splash of prosecco, lemon juice, with a white rose petal garnish. And the *Til Death Shots*. Vials filled with blood orange vodka sold as the answer to the traditional ceremonial champagne toast. Tincture guy clarifies, "And guaranteed to take your wedding to a higher level." Why not just light your guests on fire? Or blow your grandparents out of a festively decorated cannon?

I turn to Naomi to tell her all that had come of her timeline experiment was that now I wanted to uproot, overdose in the ocean, and call it a night. She calls me a dark fiancée, even darker as a wife, hands me cold water, and guides me over to a booth of alternative wedding-event designs. The most popular event themes, the woman working the booth volunteers, were anything Star Wars, retro, comic book, and Jim Henson. In her lookbook are blushing brides in creamy, lacy, long gowns, beautifully manicured hands rubbing R2D2, which could set you back $10,000. All that money made me ravenous. Luckily the spirit was hungry too. Though, where did Naomi put it? I ask her. She licks my face.

Outside, it is easy to find food—there is only one truck. Food perhaps being the most important part of a wedding celebration and here was just one vendor selling kale. This event sucked. Kale is fine, but not on weekends. Saturdays are for pizza, bagels, hotdogs. Naomi pulls out a pocketknife and threatens to cut out my tongue, Ovid style. (Jesus—she's from Ontario.) The spirit asks why it's so tough for me to see the origin of my unhappiness. She then points out that one third of the booths are photo-related. Alternative weddings are also tethered to the traditional wedding photographer, but what makes these events unique are the inclusion of photo-taking machines. If slow-motion video is too expensive, starting at $1,400, perhaps check out Drunken Pixel. The baseline, barebones price for this picture-taking apparatus, minus the props, an assortment of oversized sunglasses, clown noses, Playboy bunny ears, red and blue bandannas—for both the Bloods and the Crips—will run you $1,500. Add Quaaludes, 2015's alternative to bath salts as Elitedaily.com suggests. There's the mobile VW photobooth bus with a handmade sequin glitter backdrop to get unconventional in front of. Only $1,300 for three hours. Remember, the vehicle moves even if the backdrop stays the same, the spirit says, and I repeat after her like reading a fortune-cookie metaphor.

I'm in the bathroom, I mind-texted Naomi. *I need a break. I'm reading a newspaper article. Eighteen people in Tennessee were killed today due to hypothermia and road accidents, all weather related.*

Naomi passes me a roll of TP beneath the stall, tells me it's time for 2021, despite my protests, especially now that I recognize the game we're playing. Plus, 2021 wasn't much of a leap forward. To which the spirit says, exactly. And tells me to think harder about death before objecting.

I'm on an airplane. It's one of those big planes that fly to Dubai, and I'm in the middle row in the middle seat. The pilot has said to remain buckled in and I need to pee. All of these clues are problematic for various reasons: fears of toilet germs, fears of suicide vests. I take out my gadget to learn about the past year of my life from the latest pictures. I got divorced. I have a parakeet named Loops. Thinking outside the box appears to be the theme of 2021. Ignoring my body, I begin telling my seatmate, who's paused reading their book to express interest in my hair dye, about my big plans, about the value of debt, which only the rich get away with, but which I plan to take advantage of. My plan for 2021 was to accumulate as much debt as possible, hire young people who know technology, take out as many loans as were available, procure as many credit cards under false names, aliases, in order to live like a radical, or just the high life, like some American bigshot, before offing myself.

"What about the debt collectors? They're sharks." My seatmate is concerned.

I was no longer married. We'd had no children, it seemed from the pictures, therefore there wouldn't be anyone left, forced to pay the money back.

That said, looking at spirit Naomi, who's popped up on the screen, I am both thrilled by this idea of living the high life/offing myself, but also deeply alarmed. I miss Nick. I want little Nicks roaming the globe. The spirit tells me it's too late. I've made too many terrible decisions. She asks me if I remember hiring an interspecies communicator so that Nick and I could have sex. I do not. Naomi tells me to return to 2020, when in a fit of pandemic-induced delusional thinking I spent our savings, which wasn't saying much, on hiring an animal psychic in order to get our dog to stop barking when we tried to fuck. To be honest, I tell little ghost Naomi on the screen, livelier and more forgivable the smaller she is, I didn't see exactly what was so wrong with that thinking.

"You should have just thrown the dog in the car."

I ask Naomi if I can go home, please. She tells me we first need to go to 2015, back to the expo.

All the *Lovesick* attendees are gathered outside to listen to the event's MC, but he is struggling to figure out how to turn on his mic. Here, drink an IPA, sure tastes like you look, I humorously whisper into Naomi's ear. She does not find it amusing and wonders if I've learned anything. She gives up and takes me to 2020.

Back at home, in bed, I feel seasick. I can hear Nick washing dishes. He does this. I think he gets it from his Dutch father. Nick hasn't any pretensions about being a soft kind of guy. He doesn't pretend to throw the football around on the beach or kill animals with a bow. He's OK with making bread from scratch and adding poppy and cumin seeds.

"Where have you been?" He comes over to me, pulls my hair from my eyes, says he was wondering when I'd get out of bed and join him in the kitchen. I could tell him about the expo, about the MC's raffle, while some of us stood, sweating imprints of our thong panties into our tight denim. Los Angeles parking lots were unforgiving, he'd remember. The dark pavement absorbed heat like no other substance. I could make Nick laugh. Tell him the person with the longest beard or wearing two different socks won a t-shirt. Anyone that had on a really metal "I mean metal" bracelet got a metal bracelet. And for the lucky so-and-so not wearing underwear, they got their pick of vinyl: Kinks, Bauhaus, Dark gothic, a *Ladies Luv Outlaws* category, indie stuff, icons and legends. The winner settled on a Cat Stevens record. Wild world indeed. To which the MC pointed out to underwear-less girl, "An awesome story for Facebook!" That wasn't all. Anyone with a flask would get something. The dude with a Harry Potter tattoo would be worshipped. Any couple with matching tattoos? Nobody? You guys call that commitment!

In recollecting the day's events with my spirit friend, I kept coming back around to the giant, the person I was most drawn to, who was wobbling around on stilts and dressed in an Oogie Boogie costume from *The Nightmare Before Christmas*. I tell Nick about this looming man, and that he'd said, peering down at me, "I also do an evil clown thing." It was like the stranger knew my insides.

"You can't make that shit up," Nick says, bending over to pet our quieted dog. "Not in a million years."

Precisely. My feeling exactly. Now, please, French kiss me, hard.

Dog Star

The dog days were upon us. Before all that, it should be noted that I was an experiment, but I was not alone. I came to be inside of a world created by those that lived outside of it. I was one of those unfortunate people that from the start was not gifted eyelids when I was constructed. Not that I ever expected I would sleep in—beneath the shiny surface this place is deranged. There wasn't privacy where I lived.

The point, for now, was that the Dog Star had arrived. Though I would never see it outside of our world in nature, I understood it rose in the sky just before the late July sun and that this would be a time of drought and madness. Like things weren't bad enough. I was desperate as ever to wake up an oversized bug because the outcome in Kafka's story had already been determined. As for my outcome, it remained unknown. Yet again, I woke up myself: Honey, aspirational, defective teenager, two sweet younger brothers dreaming beside me. *They will never fear being turned into rivulets or genies*, I thought, scanning their calm boyish faces. I wanted to smother them. (I would not smother them.)

I made my way through the fluids and into the kitchen. My mother was standing next to the dishrack. All she'd ever desired was to be a citizen of the world and now look at her: she was falling apart in front of our eyes. Her materials, the ones from which she was constructed—the ones that had been promised to last longer than her mother's or father's had—were breaking down quickly in the toxic liquids which filled our world.

"Honey," my mother said to me, "your school bus is outside."

I played my part and ignored her. I was a teenager. I knew

teenage behavior. I had spent all the years leading up to this one excitedly awaiting the period of (somewhat) acceptable, by way of "expected," misbehaving to occur. My mother had really fallen into disrepair since our creators had diagnosed her as unfit. Her arms and legs were dull and patchy in places, which she attempted to hide with concealer. Her office uniform was now difficult to make out, much of the design having worn away and nobody had been hired to replace it with something fresh, as they had with those figurines they looked to more favorably. This, plus her being batshit, was the reason our creators had relocated us from our previous home to this nebulous *very special place* to be monitored like criminals.

I'll back up a bit. Who are these people? Story has it that long ago some influential individuals—which is to say our creators that existed outside in the larger world, those people who made all the decisions about what went on inside where we lived out our days—were jostled awake by an overwhelming feeling of emptiness. Unable to shake it, desperate to feel, again, on top of the world, they built a coping mechanism in the form of a translucent sphere and stuffed it with miniature configurations like me that made them happy until some malfunctioned and made them miserable, again.

I remember thinking their cruelty was breathtaking. Their attention to the specific size and nature of our inside world, their beak-like consideration of every detail, every configuration—a perfected leaf on an inedible apple tree; pink newborns suckling on a mother's cracked, blistered nipple—each assembled with a tweezer's touch. Their scope of violence was a type of immaculate violence, which touched everything inside of our world.

I looked at my mother because I was a version of my mother.

I looked away from my mother because I was a version of my mother.

I was me.

But I was also *her*—my mother—and I understood this all too well.

My mother then passed me something resembling a banana. I

peeled open the fruit, clearly stricken with some sort of disease.

"Like it's not bad enough we've been demoted to this place!" I said to the diseased banana.

"It's a fungus that kills plants by clogging their vascular system, Honey," said my mother.

"Of course," I said, instead of saying something warranted about her birthing me despite knowing I'd live an incomplete life inside of a glitchy histrionic era. (I knew she had only a little to do with this fate, but I was a teenager in need of a scapegoat.)

I covered my eyes with my hands and returned to that brief period upon waking to July's light, pre-trekking through the toxins that constituted our world, pre-mandatory mother-daughter conversation next to the dishrack. In that moment I imagined it would be the day I'd turn into something worthwhile, like an octopus. Their bodies are so soft they can squeeze through the tiniest cracks. They're the best. Or a supermodel. They're long.

"Runts, small creatures, they are not to be underestimated, Honey," my mother said. "Millions of years ago it was the puny that survived the hellscape."

My mother knew exactly what I was thinking. This was the case more and more as I grew older. Further proof the ensuing weeks would be real downers.

"Alice and I are hatching a plan to escape by transforming into reflexive forms; camouflage masters like octopuses are a single body-wide eye," I said.

"Alice is a bad influence," my mother said about my only friend, going on to play her part to ignore me.

She wasn't a fan of Alice. *Too much imagining*, she had said of Alice's shortcomings, like my mother hadn't had the totality of her youth to imagine a different outcome. Alice—fellow teenager, subsequent neighbor in the nebulous place, whose mother like my mother was batshit, which was why our families had been relocated to the area to live in surveilled matching apartments, and who like me did her best to behave harmoniously and to dress accordingly—

was perfect to me. At this stage in our so-called development, we both wore short synthetic paisley puff-sleeved mini-jumpers like good teenage girls, as we had been prescribed. Like all kids, Alice and I were expected to continue progressing, to pass through discrete units of time: infancy, adolescence, adulthood. But the truth was we went nowhere. And we were going nowhere. This we told no one, save for each other.

My younger brothers finned into the kitchen. They picked their noses and demanded goldfish since all the other boys their age had goldfish. They ate the extractions and went on to say they were starving.

"STARVING!"

My sweet brothers had devoured everything and had left nothing.

"Honey—go," my mother said, pointing again to the bus outside waiting to take me to learn.

"Right. *Education*."

Last week in school we studied Norman Rockwell's *Freedom From Want* (1943), which depicted a plentiful Thanksgiving table. It was explained to us kids that the stew we failed to make every night (because we're obligated to use cooking techniques inspired by Herodotus from the 5th century, which meant filling paunches made from animal hide and insufferably trying to light the bones beneath them) was an homage to a more bountiful and harmonious time, which was why we continually failed to make it. "I would like to point out that we're given trampolines, but we're told not to jump on them," I had said to our teacher of the endless contradictions in our world—like legitimizing Rockwell paintings and trying to cook in a snow globe.

"Don't forget this," my mother said, handing me my backpack. I hugged her. She was my mother.

The bus dropped Alice and me off at school. Before entering, we taped our mouths shut to doubly ensure we obeyed. Last week we were separated for bad behavior. Plus, we were determined to surpass our mothers in terms of accumulating additional freedoms based on performing well. Super plus, there was a chance that things would be different in a few years' time. Perhaps our world would be discovered by non-influential regular people, or perhaps our creators would die.

"These so-called *lessons* feed on a kind of perverse mixed messaging where one is expected to grow and to learn and to progress, only to suffer for it," Alice said, un-taping her mouth for a second to get out those last words.

"Honey," Alice continued when she should have kept her mouth taped shut, "we're being subjected to a purity script, which makes it a punishment script."

She went on: "God is obviously incredible, in terms of potentiality—here, there, everywhere—but there's something to be said for brevity and souls passing quickly through the night. Don't you think, Honey?"

Alice said a lot of things I failed to understand. Sometimes her personality got in the way of her developmental progress, but as usual she was on to something: those that made us had given us access to the most important texts of the time; however, indulging in them, or taking them to bed as we did with literature and philosophy could disappear you. Or have you relocated to a nebulous place on the outskirts of town, like us.

"See what I mean about perversity?"

I did.

I saw what Alice meant, and it wasn't because I didn't have eyelids. We were being tested, prodded, and warned at every turn that should we take things too far we'd pay the price.

"We were not designed to last," I said, reluctant to articulate what I held in my heart.

"Honey, you don't even have eyelids!" Alice said.

"Worse," I said, "soon we'll be expected to blow the popular twins, *The Kevins*."

"Have you seen their teeth?"

"I want to be my own kind of female," Alice said.

"I will be my own kind of teenager," I said.

"This place is a madhouse."

"What a nightmare."

"From today on we will not wear cute jumpers or blow anyone."

It's important to note that we, too, started out as fertilized eggs inside this firmament. It's important to remember that their experiment of creating us to exist in this world they had designed was a tragedy being disguised as a fresh start. It's germane to point out that infants—regardless of their construction and constitution, regardless of whether they're made from compromised materials—are still babies. And whether Alice and I were to become fully realized potential in this place or not—which we were not (females as a rule were excluded from this possibility)—like every baby, even outside of this inside place, we were promised this potential.

"Honey, I can read your mind and it's no good here," my mother said.

"Am I wrong?"

My mother gave me that sad expression, the one she toted around like a miniature toolbox at the ready to fix our problems; her face already half-destroyed by the environment. I should have felt sorry for her, about her raising us kids alone, and the right half of her face looking like melted plastic. Besides, she didn't need to say what she was about to go on to say, I already knew: I was just one figurine among hundreds, perhaps thousands, that "came to be inside of a perfect globe," our creators explained, "intended to restore mankind to a natural balance." A liquid-filled divine shape which predated recorded history; the form that made whole equal whole.

"Let's be honest, this is a bad situation," I said.

"In my day," my mother said, a sentiment she repeated often, "nobody was regularly sick. Back then our creators exercised experimental integrity. Now they come and go as they please."

My mother, herself a sensation to behold—she was an artist

to her core—began performatively chain-smoking, and propped a boombox up on her shoulder before she began bloody-murder-screaming our personal anthem—*I am doll eyes, doll mouth, doll legs, I am doll parts, bad skin, doll heart, Yeah, they really want you, they really do!*—until she collapsed on the kitchen floor.

"This was our song," I said about what felt like the end of an era, peering down into her face like a crystal ball despite knowing it was a terrible idea.

My mother could not take it anymore.

I thought: I would never be a supermodel. Never long. I would remain a figurine.

My older brother Joey (before blowing up) had warned me parents were designed to invade space and to prefer their generation before they became intolerably grumpy at the state of the world. Jesus, was that a scene—Joey blowing up. Somehow, Joey became fully realized at the age of fourteen, which was young. If it happened at all, it wasn't expected to happen until much later. With nobody else to blame, my mother blamed her mother, who'd said that from birth she knew Joey was faulty (which was to say he was trouble), and because of this he would *surely go down early*. Whoever was at fault, their head exploded. They would never be more than pieces, never a parent or a local leader. The scene was bonkers. I had to clean my brother off the glass with Windex. Windex was a joke—you try aiming spray inside a liquid filled sphere. Our creators demanded I collect each remaining fragment of Joey and make a pile of my older brother downtown in front of Sears. After, those figurines with unusually small hands—children under the age of six and the capable elderly—were tasked with skewering pieces of Joey on pikes lining our district's periphery. (We had access to modern-day alternatives, but nothing beats a pike in terms of setting the tone. Do you know what I mean?) A few days later, what remained of our family was presented with a nude gold man award. *From what I can see, it's really chintzy*, my mother had blurted.

Apparently, Joey's performance had been spot-on. *Tap. Tap. Tap*, our creators fingered the glass (creating tidal waves, mind you) and explained they would place the hefty gold-plated statue near our home for our pleasure. This period—the one involving a glistening naked gold man close by for our enjoyment—seemed like an eternity. Until the shiny nude man was moved elsewhere, it seemed to me there was no night. No peace inside. No peace for miles outside of our surveilled apartment complexes. I wrapped cloth around my eyes, because I had not been given eyelids, but nothing prevented the glimmering sheen of his gold athletic genitals from wallpapering our home.

"We've become mere playthings," I said to Alice as we moved through a very snowy downtown.

"Is there a sexual position called *crucifixion* or did I dream that?"

"Alice. Please."

Alice was one of those types where being hungry meant being grumpy and being grumpy could get us into further trouble. But who could blame her? She was employed at Taco Time. The wages were terrible. The food inedible. Nobody working there ate the food even though the managers offered employees one complimentary burrito per shift.

"The Bible says in the last days we'll become voracious lovers of ourselves," Alice said.

"Alice, I'm serious. Our creators have no restraint. None whatsoever."

These days our creators were entering our world often, and without warning, which was setting off tsunamis, blizzards, uprooting trees and houses, meticulous designs that had been deliberately installed with care. Now, pretty floating waste. Even after sump pumps drained much of the water, oil, and antifreeze, their tooling about shin-deep wreaked havoc. Chards of snow swirled for days on end if the bone chips had not been settled in advance. Our creators had their reasons. For one, they explained to us, our facial expressions needed to be imbued with a greater humanity. Sometimes they needed to break away from their daily lives in nature, which they found increasingly tedious.

"Right," Alice scoffed. "Like when they *borrow* young females to lick the rim of their magnifying goggles or their foreheads."

(They did. They had young figurines lick their sweaty foreheads.)

"Look, another one," I pointed.

Another man was hypnotized by our roundtrip train. They were hooked.

"It goes in circles. That's all the train does. Round and round."

"Their commitment is exhausting."

Alice was pissed.

"Have you forgotten yourselves?!" Alice got the man's attention by incessantly biting his shin.

"You look seriously uncomfortable," I said of his posture, hunched. Our creators were simply too big for our world. Believe me, I was all in favor of them making fools of themselves, but really, they looked ridiculous bent over like that.

"We're here because of your desire to resuscitate the integrity of the illusion! Now all you do is make messes! What's wrong with you people?"

I'd never seen Alice so distraught.

"Look, little lady, nobody on the outside has access to tinker with this kind of sordid sexy ruthless shit, not in these exact dimensions," one man said.

Crouched, holding a squirming Alice up to his eye, inspecting her figure—*flawed*—the man made sure to point out, "This is a kind of therapy! An immersive experience. A break from the fallen world. I'm desperate to be good!"

"You people are fucked," Alice said, knowing dirty language was a no-no.

Our troubles solidified Christmas Eve. Alice called me to say image was psyche when she was supposed to be wearing a red velvet dress and praying for our souls. She was tired of being taken advantage of. The perversity, the fraudulence, our so-called *existence*, so clearly assembled out of a desire to have it both ways, had reached a point not even Alice could spin.

"Honey, I hate to say it, but I'm having trouble reading. I can't keep focused on the words. I fear I've lost the meaning."

Alice had uncovered something she wasn't supposed to know. Something had entered her world that had shifted its meaning for good.

"I don't understand the image and psyche part," I said.

(I was attempting to redirect the conversation.)

"IRL a suffering Jesus cried out: *My God, my God, why have you forsaken me?* Remember?"

This struck a chord. How could I forget the lesson on Diminishing Returns? That lesson was the best.

"We live in a genre cave," Alice said. "*King Lear* is about flesh and the mind. Bodies, love, these labors cannot be trapped within a maniacal director's limits."

There must be a way out. I thought: Octopus. Octopus. Octopus. Supermodel. Supermodel. Supermodel, I anthemed, hoping to levitate elsewhere.

We told our mothers we were spending the night at the other's house. With our trekking poles we went to get hot chocolate from Starbucks. At thirteen we did not believe in Santa, but we needed hot chocolate. We held onto our Styrofoam cups, waiting to feel, and we felt nothing. Even with extra marshmallows floating on the top, little cylindrical shapes crying out for help. We dumped our cups and asked ourselves what it would be like to be Mary Magdalene today. How would she be depicted in our time?

"Portrait of a sinner?"

"Portrait of humility?"

"I can't take this," Alice said, putting on her fins and pulling me along.

Downtown looked festive. The holiday lights were up, and so was Pat Nixon's "1972 Tree," inspired by art and nature, and adorned with thousands of satin balls. We passed snowmen, Nativity scenes, the cutest little children making snow angels. On the streets, carolers were loyally dressed in shades of red and green, all the while doing their best to project their voices: *All is calm, and all is bright, round yon virgin, mother and child* in a liquid-filled spectacle. Alice pointed out the bedazzled suffocating pine trees dying slowly inside well-lit homes of the well-to-do.

"I'd like to think we could be like that one day. Well-to-do," Alice said.

"We're like those balloons that lose air slowly through one tiny unseen hole."

"We're like those Christmas lights that don't work on account of the one unidentifiable broken light."

"We're like those snow globes that show life as it's supposed to be."

"This place is unhealthy," Alice said.

Then we played rock, paper, scissors to determine who would practice giving head. I got rock. Alice got paper.

Alice took a plastic bag out of her pocket, proceeded to load the bag with stones and handed it to me.

At home, I did all I could to ignore myself, but it was too late. I was a teenager. My landline rang. My middle brother, who had reached that pivotal prepubescent age designating himself the *house phone answerer*, bear-attacked me to get on the line. Alice and I had taken things too far with our plan to transform ourselves into camouflage masters. Our papers had been discovered.

"I told you this wouldn't go over well," I said.

"Haters," Alice screamed.

Our papers, full of illustrations and anatomical descriptions of octopuses, also contained paragraphs about certain origins and first instances, i.e. formulas in sacred texts that our creators worshipped. Namely familial abuse, simulated death, the tragic-epic. Services to power, Alice and I had concluded concisely. Therefore, the discovery of our documents meant that we were in big trouble. Before static took over the line, my best friend and I came to understand that pain was proof of despair, and nothing amused our creators more than our struggling to get by. Without struggle, they said we'd just be fool-hearted trinkets making a go at it, and as they saw it that was not the fate of mankind.

"How else to explain birth? Son of man, nations, pumpkins to priests?"

"Alice, we live in a different world."

The recriminations would reveal themselves in stages, as recriminations must. First, Alice and I were prescribed *The New Testament* (again). (Which we knew exceptionally well.) We were given Xanax and tons of other unnamed pills. Our creators demanded that Alice and I voluntarily dismantle ourselves and concede.

"We will not," we said.

"Take our tongues away!" we told the fascists. "They barely work anymore as it is!"

Our tongues and navigational gear, like our fins and trekking poles, were removed. Our leads were shortened to mere inches. Ankle monitors were fastened. Our creators went so far as to confiscate our Hegel and Degas, which posed no significant threat. None whatsoever.

"Oh, now I'll get to sleep in!" I said to zero fanfare.

The extent of our world was breathtaking. There was no end.

Our mothers did their best. "Kids these days," they said, appealing for a lighter punishment, arguing that in the past mothers had some measure of control when it came to handling matters concerning their own.

Once batshit, always batshit, I thought about our mothers, whom I loved but who stood no chance against our creators.

Alice and I spent our last night in the stadium, repenting. Our fellow figurines filled the stands to witness our damnation. Who could blame them? There was no entertainment inside of our world. Our creators, who fortunately had decided to remain outside, wore side lights, like those used in chiaroscuro art, and headlamps, to better see what was taking place. Our mothers were present. As a gesture of good will, they had been given longer leads so they could be there. They sat idle. Their mouths agape; soggy paper bags with eye holes over the tops of their heads, and showcasing solidarity posters.

"Hilarious," Alice signed to me.

It was so true. Our mothers were hilarious.

Per routine, our local leaders would now need to determine our punishment.

"What do you girls say for yourselves?" they asked.

"Illusions are tricky," Alice signed.

They turned to look at me, sharply.

Honey, my mother thought, soggy bag over the top half of her head: At least we're doing this in the stadium and not in the clinic. That dismal, sad, concrete building that offered to help women, was not a building any female should enter.

If she could read my mind, I could read hers.

"What she said," I signed and pointed at Alice.

The incriminating questions would continue, but I'd checked out by then. I was thinking back to a day in school when our class watched for hours this video of a birthday party for former Tyco CEO Dennis Kozlowski's wife, thrown on the island of Sardinia, which featured an ice sculpture of Michelangelo's *David* spewing vodka from his penis, a cake shaped like a woman's breasts with sparklers on top, and guests wearing togas and tight briefs, dancing to a performance by Jimmy Buffett. There was a message somewhere in all of it.

I scanned the stadium. There was so much light in the space—like an explosion. On the screens lining the dome were images of demons and furtive angels as if they wanted a part in an altogether different motif, but mostly demons. Where I lived, girls were girls until they were mothers or went missing or simply disintegrated. I prayed, knowing nothing would change the horrors of this world. I saw my mother smile. She could read my mind, which had told her she was my hero. Her body, a fraction of what it had been, a sign of what was to come.

Alice and I were banished from society for an undisclosed amount of time. We were staked inside a fogbound tent that teetered on the edge of a tall cliff and overlooked a roaring sea. There was a lighthouse, unwavering in the distance. Nothing more. No views of residential or commercial areas. As was custom, one by one, others were permitted to stop by with offerings: fortune cookies, red-and-white-striped paper straws. Even some well-to-do figurines came by. They had the best stuff—quality junk. And in some irrational state, the one where Alice and I convinced ourselves we would be OK, we decided to hold onto the fancy items with their original tags so that we might later sell them. Our mothers were the last to visit for the very reason that it was hardest for them.

"Honey, there's nothing more to give," my mom said, pulling up her shirt to peek at her sunken breasts.

I hadn't realized they'd sunken.

"Nothing more to be done," Alice's mom said, her figure—armless.

"Sure," we signed.

We were thirteen. It wasn't a secret we'd run out of room.

For a time, Alice and I got into our updated lives staked inside a tent above the roaring sea. We swore like seamen. Scratched at what was left of our vaginas, said: "Nothing about our world was different from any other spectacle," and turned our attention to a new plan, which was to build a worldwide white noise machine. We figured if we found a way to penetrate the atmosphere, we could use the satellites in space to blanket Earth in white noise. This had the ability to impact everything. This was a better, more permissible use of time than entertaining correlations between birthing and pumpkins. Or hoping to morph into an octopus.

A dank stillness settled in. Increasingly disoriented, ever bone-weary, Alice had me unfasten her stapled eyelashes from either side of her face. "Let the beasts fall over my eyes like a lid," she'd said. She stopped responding to me. In my head, I began to formulate these thoughts, which I used all my might to focus on. I imagined

Alice was in nature. I thought about Kafka's Gregor, his trembling little bug legs, and pictured him gazing out his childhood window, desperate to recognize the view. Whenever I'd had the chance to see through our world to the world outside, to be that close to the glass to glimpse something else, I saw nothing but a marble of an image. I held Alice and wished we'd remained savage, carnal babies. Babies were never punished or destroyed, not even in our world.

Alone, I would trace with my fingers the canoe carvings Alice had made into my forearms. There was this one little netted "window" on the roof like a skylight, through which I'd watch the patch of sky move within the geometry of the fabric. I pictured Alice's face like a handheld mirror and began to record what I knew of her with the tape recorders our mothers had left us. The alternative was to suggest Alice did not exist. That none of us existed. And nobody should be expected to be OK with that.

Eventually I was allowed to return. I was hired part-time at an up-and-coming beauty supply chain. I sold eyebrow brushes and lip balm and was also employed in the customer service department for a company selling direct-to-consumer mattresses. There were now tons of stores selling "unique" mattresses, each with the same promise that guaranteed the identical outcome. How could that be?

In the space of my mind that remained my own, I invited Alice into my delirium. Like today, I was checking out at Safeway, loading an assortment of canned goods onto the conveyor belt, when I saw Alice, clear as day. Please, stay with me. It was our Alice. She was in infant form. Primal baby Alice in a porcelain tub, thinking, which kept being misdiagnosed as arrhythmia. She was premature, a shallow green, glowing and frightening the nurses around her. Nurses clutched their chests, and not because of Alice's proximity to death, but because of her ideas. Her father was there; I could tell he was her father because he was made from the same dense materials. Her mother was not. Alice wouldn't latch to her breasts to feed; our creators had her removed and put out of sight. Expressive, radical-beast-baby Alice wanted to live a wondrous life, but had second thoughts after taking stock of her surroundings. There was a clock on the pristine wall she could read, even with those heavy eyelashes that covered her eyes, tiny as needle pricks. Alice wondered why our tendency when considering matters of time was to emphasize the hour. The minute hand was longest, yet the increment being measured was narrower. Why were they called "hands" to begin with?

I lingered there until I was told to hurry my cheap, bent ass up. The grocery line had grown out of control and agitated.

"Bad weather is coming," said others.

"You!" figurines demanded. "Yes—you, Honey! Move along!"

Next, I flashed to Alice as an old woman. Her face had aged and in doing so had become more recognizable. More Alice. Layers of Alice. Alice volcano. Just listen. Don't turn away. The afternoon sun was coming through the interstices of the sphere's glass, casting a soft yellow hue over our world inside. It was summer or merely scorching. Hard to know for sure. Alice wore a brown linen pantsuit; one hundred percent linen. The fabric was soft, as if it had dressed women for centuries. She was comfortable, even in her underwear, which from the time of puberty was a big issue. There was a celebration. I knew because my mother was there, untethered, handing out condoms and shiny party hats. Batshit as ever. God, I loved her. Alice was relaxed, sitting on a wrinkled blanket on the dirt, in the middle of the day, uninterested in what would come next. Her friends surrounded her. Each, a different size and shape. I saw vegetables and fruits, most of them torn and badly bruised. Nobody noticed. The flavors were sensational; peach juice dribbled every which way. I didn't hear waterfalls, feel mosquitos bite, or smell conifer trees, but they existed. Alice—ravenous in nature. Alice—expansive, laughing hysterically, cheese gooey from the heat. Her arms, legs, and belly, spreading to every corner like spilled milk.

The Craftsman

It was wrong and weird, but the man and the woman felt they had little choice. From their basement apartment, in what was considered an in-law unit, they listened through the thin walls as the vibrating alarm went off in the main house above them. Afterward, the man and the woman lay unpleasantly awake, wondering why the female who lived upstairs set her alarm for 5:30 a.m. if she wasn't planning to get out of bed for another few hours. They were dumbfounded. Not one of the three young people now living in the Craftsman above had a schedule. The three of them did as they pleased. How could that be?

Exhausted and unable to go back to sleep, the man and the woman imagined what it was the young girl upstairs was doing with herself in that big old house. What was she doing with her live-in rocker boyfriend during that time, the time between waking up and finally getting out of bed? He certainly had no place to be either. And what was the other roommate, the one they sympathetically referred to as "Third Wheel," what was he doing while all this other doing was taking place? He had no place to be at 5:30 in the morning, none of them did, not at their ripe age, not in sunny Los Angeles, not with their limited qualifications. The three twentysomethings living above intrigued the man and the woman.

Often, as the man and the woman lay in bed, having been woken prematurely, they pictured the young girl upstairs rising slowly out of her soft sheets, deliberately putting on nude stockings one fit leg at a time, although they conceded it didn't make much sense given the heat wave. It was far too hot for stockings. She wasn't even thirty! Her young skin glistened like polished silver; it glowed like aftermath. How old was she anyway? Did anyone even wear stockings anymore? The man and the woman living below felt outdated as they readied for work.

Sometimes the man and the woman envisioned the young girl turning over onto her other side to face her indie-rock boyfriend, who was nice enough, but not outright friendly like some his age were. They noted this about him. His uncouthness. They imagined the young girl sidled up to him, brushing aside his wispy dirty-blond hair to make room for a peck on his once twice-pierced ear. Perhaps she laid out a pulsing of pecks, with those perky, pouty lips she heavily glossed, the ones that accounted for her relative success starring in a Disney series about a girl finding her way in advertising—in New York City of all places. What did she, the young girl, know about city living? What did any of them really know? The three of them had just arrived there, fresh out of college, the man and the woman thought to themselves as they tidied up their small basement apartment.

The above sequence, the man and the woman presumed, was what led to the rough sex they overheard at different hours in the day. The young couple above had no routine whatsoever, zero consistency. They didn't stick to morning sex or evening sex, the young couple just did it whenever. Whenever, can you imagine? If given the opportunity, the man and the woman living below might have devised an alternative university schedule; they had no desire to hear the banging coming from the main house above. Had the young couple displayed any regularity, any detectable pattern, the man and the woman could have avoided the concurrent and awkward overlaps. Why must they be around to hear what was happening in the Craftsman? A deep, leisurely, escalating groan, followed by *wack wack wack*, then a heavy *bang*, like an iron church bell had fallen, cracking a monumental marble altar. It wasn't right. It just wasn't.

There were other sounds that came from the main house. At random times in the day, it was common to hear the young girl scream, a Hitchcock-like scream, the security of a home interrupted by an intruder—running bath water, glistening steak knife, terrified, buckling, at the final moment no audio, just an image absent of sound. At times the man and the woman wondered if the young actress was really in distress. Should they call the police? But the girl upstairs was a professional, and they figured that since her family-friendly TV show was canceled that she must have been preparing for auditions. That had to be it. Though how did Third Wheel, the extra young one living among the unfazed couple, feel about all this pleasure? Or violence?

From below, the man and the woman got ready for their long commute to work. They had concerns about the main house. But the man and the woman chose not to be troubled by the actions upstairs. From what they knew of the young couple, it would seem congruous that they would be dispassionate about knocking over vintage lamps since they themselves refurbished the second-hand items. Reserve your concerns, they told themselves. Happiness wasn't in itself a disorder.

If that wasn't enough, there were the abrasive sounds of the young girl's heels tromping indelicately over their nicely polished wooden floors, originals. Little regard they seemed to have for that fact. It was not how the man and the woman would have treated those floors. *Clack clack clack*, the young actress traipsed from the bathroom to the kitchen to the bedroom, back to the kitchen and back to their bathroom, where she spent most of her time. She was beautiful. No doubt about it. Funny, neither the man nor the woman ever saw the young girl in them, the heels, but they imagined they added significant height to her compact but well-proportioned frame. True, they conceded in the sanctity of their basement apartment, all actors were short, but the young girl above in the main house, she was really truly short.

It got the man and the woman thinking. The young actress' height meant that the guy she starred alongside during her short-lived TV series must have been super short. Her size made the man and the woman feel discourteous. If ever they ran into her, they'd loosen the lock on their knees so as not to seem hierarchical—they were liberals, for Christ's sake. The man and the woman tried to see the world from the young girls' perspective. They concluded that they were too tall, too tall for fame, though they agreed that they weren't in Los Angeles for fame, even if at one point in time they'd considered leading a life in the arts, long ago before it all felt trivial. Perhaps it was time to relocate. The neighborhood was indeed changing. But their basement apartment was such a deal. The man and the woman would never find a deal like that again in the city.

Once, the man and the woman ran into the young couple unloading a bruised Olivetti typewriter and a reel-to-reel, the kind the man and the woman had used years ago to build their early careers as sound-scape artists. Sound-scape artists. Ha! The idea of it now seemed preposterous. The young boyfriend said of his acquisitions, This shit doesn't look like much but I'll make it into something real, you watch. Right, *real*, the man and the woman thought, leaving unsatisfied through their gravel driveway, heading back into their small but dearly loved basement apartment.

One time, the man and the woman ran into the boyfriend at the epicurean coffee shop down the street that people drove miles to get to. With nothing to talk about, they felt it was appropriate to inform the young boyfriend about the mail—their glossy magazines, credit card bills, and well-meaning European postcards were spilling out of the shared mailbox. It was all over the sidewalk. Not one of the three of them had noticed? Selfishness offended the man and the woman, but nothing like the offense of litter. Because of this the man and the woman had decided to put their overflowing items in plastic bags. They had hung them on the moribund tree—Did he or his sweet young girlfriend see them? they asked the intrepid boyfriend. Did they see the plastic bags full of magazines they'd left nicely hanging on the tree? There wasn't time for newspaper reading, the boyfriend said, when he finally stopped drinking his coffee to answer. Oh, the man and the woman said simultaneously, observing the boyfriend as he winked, like a mosquito had landed in his eye, at the female barista who wore a bold gold necklace: HELL. The rocker was up. The man and the woman could tell. If there was one thing they knew for certain about the three young people living upstairs in the Craftsman, it was that they knew prescription meds. First clue? The boyfriend had mistaken fashion magazines for the newspaper. Second? He was picking at his cuticles in rapid succession. The man and the woman refused to worry about it—he wasn't their son.

As a rule, if the man and the woman came into contact with the three of them, they didn't hang long, just long enough to see how Third Wheel's screenplay was shaping up, or how the young couple's refurbishing projects were going. Other subjects included the young couple's trip to Burning Man and a wedding in Palm Springs. The man and the woman were reluctant. It could have been their age, but they didn't want to spoil the mood—they couldn't believe people still went to Burning Man since it had become an expensive event for sellouts and soul-seekers. The man and the woman couldn't wrap their minds around the idea that Palm Springs had again become the embodiment of vacation, and that young people yearned to spend hours drifting blissfully by, splashing around in silky pools. We might be old, they conceded in the safety of their bed below. Palm Springs?

Unfailingly on trash day, the man and the woman ran into Third Wheel, as he committedly moved the trash and recycling bins onto the street for pick up. He was so trustworthy. Other than delivery and Boca burgers, what did the three young people consume? The man and the woman worked hard to suppress their curiosities about their upstairs neighbors. It was not their business.

On other days, when they unexpectedly bumped into Third Wheel, he was always alone. Nevertheless, he mentioned having a girlfriend. She's nearby, he would say, like around the corner, he'd say, gesturing a ways off. Even though the man and the woman never asked. It was as though Third Wheel was saying—I'm not really the guy you think I am. But he was, he was exactly that guy: a helper, slushy shy, and undeniably considerate. He must have been the nicest guy there ever was. Third Wheel was heartbreakingly genuine. Genuine, he was genuine and trustworthy, the man and the woman told each other, grading stacks of papers in their basement apartment. They didn't understand why he stayed with the others for as long as he did. But it wasn't their concern.

The young actress was never out there at night when her boyfriend and Third Wheel drank beers and played long games of chess. From their basement apartment the man and the woman wondered why the young girlfriend didn't join them—was there something about chess that unsettled her? Instead, the girlfriend could be seen sauntering down the stairs from their second-floor bedroom in a silk robe, a lightly shaded pink silk robe to fetch him, her rocker boyfriend. How long could the three of them live like in a movie, especially one so poorly written? Forever, that's what the man and the woman thought in the dark light about the value of writers being further diminished. They could live in a poorly written movie forever.

One day, there was a light knock on the door to their basement apartment. It was the young girl from the main house. The man and the woman invited her inside, but she said she was fine. The actress had heard from a friend, whose father taught at the university where the man and the woman were employed, that they were professors. Thing is, the young actress said, I'm crafting a riddle to explain how I'm feeling. And to prepare for an upcoming role, she said, nothing major, just a small part for an underground theater company that no one will ever see. The girl from the Craftsman was thinking that the two of them, being an older married couple, and both professors, might be just the right people to tell her if her riddle was any good. The young girl cleared her throat: How was it that living in a consistently warm climate, in a place that prides itself on seasonal well-being, such as Los Angeles, I experience so much internal suffering?

The girl looked down at her bare feet, her painted mauve toes pointed inward toward the other foot, forming a triangle. Neither the man nor the woman had an answer. Open-mouthed, the man and the woman loosened their knees. I know it's bad, the young girl said. I'll continue to work on it, she said, as she walked down the man and the woman's gravel path and out through their gate.

Letting Snails Go

Birdy got busted less than a day back upstate. Busted by Margaret in front of Sunfrost Farms grocery store, collecting a kitten from a shoebox that read: *I couldn't feed them. They're always hungry.* Margaret was visibly discontent, twisting her gingham button-down shirt with her ring finger, demanding to know why she hadn't heard Birdy was back in town. She didn't like being out of the loop: Had Birdy decided to finally join the real world on Facebook? Had she contacted Darlene? She'd better be attending their twentieth high school reunion. Darlene would require an immediate response if Birdy was to reserve her spot. In the flurry of organizing, it had become one of those "or else" kind of situations.

"You know how Darlene can be," Margaret warned.

It was growing dark. The rain splashed against the moving cars. It seemed each summer became rainier upstate and though the region knew bears and experienced snowy winters, people had difficulty with the increasingly heavy rain. Birdy sat dressed for her high school reunion in the yard underneath the palapa her father had built after seeing an advertisement in a travel magazine for the Bahamas. She watched the cars drive poorly in the rain, sipping on a bent can of Miller Lite (all her father had), clipping at her split ends with a pair of dull scissors. She got buzzed and tightly braided her hair. Not a loose side braid like she wore in high school, but a tight braid, a corseted crown of hair that snaked around the circumference of her skull, stretching out the skin on her forehead like a map. Wearing her hair this way made her feel awake and fresh in her body, like being submerged in water, like getting a splinter.

Her father was standing at the kitchen counter, reading obituaries.

It was his evening ritual: crack a Miller Lite, decide from a stack of boxed meals which appealed most, and read the obits. Everything was just as it had been since she'd last visited: the dishwasher was broken; the clocks were set to the wrong hour; the fridge was empty save for a few crusty hot dog condiments. Her bedroom was still being used to store damp furniture and moldy photo albums, all of which were the result of the ghost: A seven-year-old boy who'd drowned in the '80s, everyone's least favorite decade. The ghost boy apparently lived in the laundry room and had issues with water, which was why the ghost liked to make trouble with the pipes, because of *his water issues*.

After her run-in with Margaret at Sunfrost, Birdy thought about calling Darlene, but the two of them hadn't spoken in over twenty years. Darlene transferred to their Catholic high school from her boarding school after she'd been caught selling her parents' uppers and credit cards. She was a force, Darlene. She demanded unwavering loyalty. She regularly listed the characteristics about each girl in the group she found to be intolerable, which could take hours. Trouble began when Birdy got ballsy. Sophomore year in front of the girl group, a fed-up Birdy told Darlene her look was outdated. (She could have just called her a bitch.) It was time Darlene update her look, put a gun to her head, pull the trigger, and call the new look: *Jackson Pollock Visits Sarasota for the First Time*. Certainly that would *wow* people, not to mention you'd be worth more millions, Birdy had said to the group of girls, formerly known as her friends.

Birdy had chosen Sarasota for its promise of an eternal ocean, the intoxicating smell of the sea, access to unlimited air conditioning, and because that's where her mother had met her fourth husband, a jewel of a man, a retired real estate agent known for his protruding gut and his direct, no-nonsense sense of humor. (She'd always thought real estate agents dealt in real estate for life.)

Birdy's time in the group had been short, but she'd managed to make a few of Darlene's exclusive slumber parties where she saw things—like how the rich lived—and experienced things—like her relationship with Margaret shifting. Once, outside on her expansive terrace, Darlene had demanded protection against the draft—a shawl, a coat, something—rubbing her arms to indicate her pressing need for warmth or someone's careful touch. Birdy offered to run inside to grab her a coat. In the back of Darlene's walk-in closet she found so many coats. She also found Margaret tucked away, stripped down to her underpants, her hand moving over her panty-covered vagina, her head strained back like a mare.

"Please," Margaret had whisper-begged.

Birdy assured her that she would not say anything to Darlene. And that there was no shame in masturbating, though Birdy knew that wasn't accurate. People delighted in shaming other people, especially when it came to pleasure, especially women and pleasure, especially in high school. Though, as Birdy would later find on reaching adulthood, that wasn't accurate either. Shaming women and their pleasure would go on indefinitely. Birdy's father had given her a bumper sticker for her eighteenth birthday: *Guilt is the gift that keeps on giving.* The sentiment had a way of resonating as the years passed.

In the wet high school parking lot, Birdy watched some snails inch along and imagined that she was a part of their slow-motion routine. Snails, she thought, both focused and meandering—how fantastic, such that she snatched a few up to further covet. She also ran into her ex there, JP, short for Jon Paul, the Catholic school jokes eternal, eternally un-amusing. His red shoelaces were untied; now all she'd think about for the rest of the night was when and where JP would trip over his soaked red shoelaces. He smiled, said *hi*, and asked her if she was still working in the city as a puppeteer. She was still working as a puppeteer, as long as her projects remained inspirational. A string of Yelpers had recently taken issue with what they called her "morbid themes," insisting puppetry was for children's birthday parties, and the occasional bachelor and bachelorette party. The things bachelors and bachelorettes asked Birdy to do with her puppets had her later burning them in effigy. (She would not share this information with the Yelpers, who'd simply needed to be assured of their rightness. She needed to stay in business. The city was expensive.)

Birdy's latest project was modeled on Batesian mimicry; in order to survive, an otherwise harmless organism must learn how to mimic a noxious predator. She told JP she'd been stuck developing a major combat scene set to take place between the two central characters, both female. It wasn't combat, exactly, since neither would have weapons traditionally associated with warfare. Instead, they would need to rely on their ability to adapt behaviorally, mastering observation and emulation. One of the two characters was a wealthy brunette loosely based on Veronica from *Archie Comics*. The other was a blond middle-class girl, next-door type, loosely based on Betty of the same comic book. Birdy was at a standstill about which of the two would win. Someone would need to suffer, to perish. She revised that sentiment—much too dark, she noted. Earlier that evening she'd asked her father what she should do about the ending and the toilet started running. *The ghost*, her father explained.

It was packed and discernibly muggy inside the auditorium. Their high school wasn't known to splurge, especially on alumni, but there was an actual deejay instead of some high sprite swiveling his eyes around, lip-syncing along to Greatest Hits of Dead People.

"JP! Birdy!" Margaret called out. Nothing slipped by Margaret.

At the spiked cherry-punch bowl, Margaret asked Birdy if she'd ever hired an animal communicator; perhaps she should consider it since she'd decided to take on the responsibility of raising a kitten that would eventually become a cat. Another woman at the reunion commented that the proper term was *animal psychic*, leading to a debate about whether a psychic only looked to, or toward the future, and Margaret insisting that in order to predict, look toward, or to the future, one must also consider the past. Everyone said "duh" and moved on to talk about the juicier topic of gender. Ladling boozy cherry punch into plastic cups, Margaret and the other woman went on to discuss how successful women resented being seen as male clones, and whether Birdy should remain childless or *sneak* in children before menopause. Birdy politely excused herself; she had to change her tampon.

In the bathroom, Birdy removed from her pocket the two snails she'd borrowed from the parking lot earlier. She put them inside of her mouth. She let them slide around, along the ridges of her teeth, her salivary glands, and underneath her tongue. She let them compete for space, because that's what civilization was good at. She thought: *Like you, Snail, I too want to go unnoticed. I too need to learn to self-edit.* Washing her hands, stopping before carelessly grabbing a paper towel from the dispenser, Birdy considered self-preservation. It was pouring outside. The window to her Honda was left open in the parking lot. The fabric of the car seats would be soaked through by now. Boozy cherry punch's fault, she let her mind wander, trace and outline the Atlantic, let her mind go where it wished, reach that previously uninhabitable mental space, dirty bathroom, dirty thoughts: *People have fucked in here, in this very bathroom.*

Birdy's thoughts turned to her ex, JP. Her father had always been fond of him. *Fond* was her father's word, and he used it often to describe the things he admired, which were few: low-fat boxed microwavable meals, raw talent, coupons with worthy savings, general decency, like waiting your turn in line, and not running red lights in most circumstances. (Emergencies were emergencies.) Her father was a man of habits, something he'd learned from being in the army. Birdy came to see this part of him as a relief and not as stultifying, which was the characterization her mother, with her new husband in Florida, had perpetuated. Her father liked JP because he would empty the trash before leaving their house, and no one had to ask him to do it. He did it without provocation. Her father still brought it up, all these years later.

Margaret entered the bathroom. Birdy was picking at the hairs on her arm. Margaret said something about Birdy's morbid tendencies, and how she had the name of a good therapist. Margaret, like Darlene, was all for show. But Margaret could be kinder. She strapped kindness on like dynamite even if there were occasions when it didn't fit. And unlike Darlene, Margaret was not rich. Margaret was like Birdy. She was from the woods. JP was also from the woods. Darlene then entered the space like punctuation, shiny silver nails to parallel her silver patent-leather shoes, a giant button on her chest indicating her principal role on the welcoming committee. Birdy took the two snails out of her mouth and put them on the bathroom counter.

"Jesus fucking Christ, Birdy!" Darlene screamed, hitting the counter with her fists. Birdy safely moved the snails to the linoleum floor.

Margaret and Darlene got over it when they saw themselves. They stared at their sculpted reflections in the mirror, and the other's, and in tandem applied lip-gloss: top lip, bottom lip, blot, blot. It was like they remembered nothing about their general disdain for each other, or for anyone else. Birdy admired them. Whether they didn't remember the details, or whether they remembered them precisely, it wasn't important. They got by, moved forward and looked good doing it. Their makeup sufficiently touched-up, Margaret and Darlene agreed it was time to top off their refreshments. The reunion would soon run out of booze, and they were there to just barely remember high school and get wasted. The drinking rules were different upstate, and the weather being what it was meant people would be letting loose. Darlene knew the drill. She'd written the night's program herself, and more guests were sure to arrive, especially those that hadn't RSVP'd. Not to mention the economy was tanking.

Birdy eyed the sentiments etched on the bathroom stalls: *Jenn loves John and John loves Jenn 4-reel & 4-eva!!!* to the more complex, *I finally brought my Sharpie to school, but I have nothing to say.* She came to realize she'd hand the two female leads in her puppetry project a stalemate. (Her best thinking happened in bathrooms.) Why not end on a figurative expression? It would be a positive if she were to like more people, be like more people. If she believed that all the babies in the world were cute, but she didn't find that to be the case. Some babies were flat out ugly. The wet seat in her Honda was her punishment. By now her father would be in the living room, covered up in a blanket, snoozing to a loud MSNBC program, several empty cans of beer by his side. Birdy pictured him getting to know the kitten she'd retrieved from the box, when the seven-year-old ghost boy living in the laundry room popped into her head. Would he be stuck there forever?

"Birdy? You there?" It was JP. His words hung there, articles drying on a clothesline.

"Maybe," she said. "*Sometimes*."

It didn't take long before they found themselves sitting side by side on the cool bathroom floor. JP repositioned himself. He asked Birdy what she wanted. She said she wasn't sure, but that she'd be sure to let him know when she was. He said: *Let's see where this goes*. Birdy knew that saying that was like saying nothing. It no longer bothered her. She thought back to a period in time when JP would say things like: *Been missing you*, *been thinking of you*, conveniently leaving out *I*. She asked if he was still married. He said *No*. She told him she needed to watch him watch her touch herself without him touching himself, and if he couldn't handle that then he should get out of the girl's bathroom.

Birdy did a bit of shifting around, too. She was trying out G-strings, but despite the hassle-free ads depicting fun-loving women holding margaritas, jumping up and down on trampolines, they weren't for her. JP drew closer. It wasn't cloyingly transparent. Twenty years earlier his hands would have already been down her pants, but they were grown-ups now. It seemed he was capable of more. Mortality *was* different. Nothing could change the fact that death was nearer. Birdy was the one putting her father to bed, plugging in the nightlight so he could find his way in the dark. She chopped the wood for winter and brought it into the shed. She brushed his hair, which he'd let grow long. It was Birdy that put his hair in a pony for him. She pulled his socks on over his hammertoes, and tied his shoelaces since he couldn't easily bend over.

Deadlocked in their high school bathroom, Birdy touched herself.

JP watched her closely, sometimes his eyes watered. She did not find this endearing but perhaps that was expecting too much from the situation. They held eye contact and smiled. She asked him to squeeze her body parts. Away from the music and the crowded punch bowl, the two snails gradually advanced across the checkered linoleum. The smaller of the two slowly inched forward, the other followed. Birdy and JP took their time sitting there. If they needed more time, they'd pull the fire alarm. *Is this reality?* The question was etched on the bathroom stall but by whom was unknown.

"How are you?" he asked.

"I'm learning," Birdy answered.

Encounter Beach

I learned about the intimacy travel package during a Creole cooking class. My cooking partner mentioned it just after her small dog jumped up on the counter, snatching both the sausage I had been cutting and a bite of my thumb. My partner consoled me: "Pope didn't mean any harm. He was after the meat." I didn't own any animals, but the dog's actions seemed reasonable, and so I nodded my head acceptingly. She leaned in and whispered in my ear that she'd been to a place known as the Cape as part of a travel package that focused on intimacy, a package available exclusively to females. I agreed not to mention the dog bite and she continued. "The travel guide running the program is a delightfully sensitive man, capable of converting the most uptight of people."

Immediately I excused myself and called up Margie to tell her that we had an inside connection to a discreet program. She was thrilled by the chance to leave town and be part of a group, especially one that catered to those of us looking to connect. Margie and I had both moved with our successful husbands to Palace Waterfall, a community of identical two-story houses that lined the Massachusetts Bay. The architects envisioned Palace Waterfall as a respite from a world full of naysayers. The advertisements suggested that the new community was to be a place of prestige and unity. Yet the people who occupied this development were unable to hear the sound of water even when it was located directly next to them. They referred to the sound of water as "reverb." A silent moment never passed in this community. I mostly kept to myself.

Jim picked me up from class and on our way home he talked to me about averages, and when I didn't respond his eyes darted suspiciously up and down my figure. I clutched my thumb tightly to prevent excess bleeding, my hand resting on my lap, wrapped in a paper napkin from my cooking partner's purse. I felt chilled. I need to tend to this, I thought, although I felt little pain. It was only when we pulled into the driveway that Jim appeared to notice. Looking directly at me, he asked, "What's the point if you suffer that easily?" and opened his car door to exit.

On the drive to the Cape, Margie talked about her children and said I should be grateful that I hadn't any. She told me that she had grown up being called a mule. "How do you think that would make a person feel?" she asked herself, in a voice sure of the right answer. I thought to ask her why a mule, but it wasn't necessary to be impolite. Margie put her hand on mine as the traffic on the freeway came to a standstill. Gripping it tightly, she said, "A seemingly lost woman wielding a machete does more than suggest something." I shook my head in a way that indicated my consensus. For the rest of the drive we listened to *The Real Thing*, by Tom Stoppard, while Margie practiced her self-introduction for our fellow travelers, soon to be our close friends. It was early evening when we arrived.

Once settled in at the hotel, Margie and I went to the dining hall to meet the others in the group, who had begun assembling around a large table. Our travel guide appeared, and, following a small bow, presented himself as our temporary man-slave, which received light laughter and applause. He handed each of us a yellow rose, explaining that it was a gesture of friendship. Luckily, Margie had agreed to take on the role of interlocutor and introduce us both. She'd say her name and stick out her hand. The group seemed eager for contact and admitted to being nervous about what was expected at the Cape. Margie was flawless; she never erred reciting the bio we had diligently rehearsed, and her confidence seemed to have a soothing effect on everyone. I was grateful she was willing to volunteer my personal information, which allowed me to maintain my preferred state, silence. The food was bland but our travel guide assured us that it would improve as the program adjusted itself to the venue.

He explained that the locals, who evidently were our chefs, weren't "tickled" by visitors. They saw visitors as cold, mindless thieves, out only for themselves. But as the program moved forward and began to gain momentum, the locals would grow more tolerant of our willful naivete. Margie said she understood, concluding, "No right-minded person likes strangers in their backyard, making messes and leaving them for the bears to sort out."

When the introductions ended, I returned to my room to call home. Again, Jim questioned me about my intentions in leaving for the Cape. "The house is unreasonably quiet without someone to talk to," he said. He sounded exhausted from what seemed genuine loneliness. Certainly I was to blame for the poor planning. Shortly after I hung up the phone, Margie knocked on my door to ask if I'd like to join a preliminary game of charades. I politely declined. That night I dreamed of snacks: bags filled with whole boiled and salted potatoes that were force-fed to me by a drag queen. The drag queen shrilled at me to stand up straight, while savagely licking off her mahogany lipstick with her thick pink tongue. I woke up distressed, starving, a puddle of drool on my pillow, and luckily discovered a bag of trail mix tucked away in my belongings.

The next day at orientation, our travel guide gave us an overview. "The Cape is a stretch of sand between tides that do not connect. Visitors return to this place and they do it often. It is believed that this, in part, is what sets off the locals." Our travel guide introduced the term "beauty vernacular" for the local speech, and said that as visitors we must not lay any claim to it. As visitors we must create our own speech.

"This is how folks such as us manage to stay comfortable between all this water," he explained. "As participants in the program you will be required to create a uniquely effective form of communication. Communication is essential to the success of the program."

The travel package included a system of exercises and activities to ensure we would reach our goals. These activities were designed to identify pleasure and foster commitment, our travel guide explained;

as a result, we would become better communicators and closer to our bodies. After orientation, he divided us into groups, recommending we get to work and be prepared to present our findings to the program. Margie and I belonged to group B because we had arrived second. Our first assignment was to administer our own version of "vernacular testing" by attempting to form a consensus between sensations, pictures, and words. Our group went out to evaluate roadkill in order to discover pleasure as it relates to horror.

The presentations occurred in the hotel's meeting room, a formal convention hall without windows and with many rows of brown plastic chairs. The room was painted a soft yellow hue, and I imagined that it had been painted this way to soften the blow of simply being present, such as conferences or family reunions. The walls were lined with framed inspirational sentiments, yet many people had left this room unhappy, possibly penniless. Despite clear attempts at cordiality on the part of the hotel, the room possessed a deep emptiness. Before I could escape, Margie walked to the front of the room and presented our findings:

"Group B has decided to call our test 'Back to Life.' The experiment measured the depth of our desires based on our vocal responses when passing roadkill by car. The severity of want was measured by the volume of our groaning. To this volume we attached value, since value is at the root of pedagogy and the body. Dead deer elicited the highest level of yearning; our sympathies grew wilder for deer than for any other dead thing splayed out on the road. Our groaning increased in both volume and frequency when we passed dead deer, and almost instantly our group reached out to comfort each other by touch. Our desire was for these long, thin, strong, swift creatures to return. Return to life, to the forest, so that we might be relieved of the guilt of passing them by."

We received praise all around; even our travel guide called it the best test he'd witnessed in years.

Weekly massages were a perk included in the travel plan. Each participant was assigned a specialist who gave lessons about relieving tension in various parts of the body. It was required that we practice massage on each other. By learning how to receive pleasure, I learned about possibility. This exchange of generosity provided a way to become closer to the others in the program. In the evenings, I'd try calling Jim but he'd never answer. He'd leave messages in the afternoons when he knew I'd be away. Struggling to connect was characteristic of our union and therefore I wasn't alarmed. In fact, I started to envision him out at the movies, taking long walks through the park at sunset. All of these he deserved, and I longed for his happiness. Margie and I became very close, spending the majority of our time together on the Cape. She slept in the room next to mine, which allowed us to talk late into the night when group sessions ended. We took to recounting the stories of our lives over glasses of pink wine and the peanut butter-filled pretzels her daughter sent us in the mail. During the day, we strolled along the edge of the bay in silence. Margie wasn't pleased with her marriage; she said her children begged her to divorce. We both felt that our mothers had never been taught to be happy, and I had the feeling that our grandmothers hadn't either. The Cape was a special place: one devoid of apathy, that made us feel differently, which was to say allowed us to feel. The local people were connected to the land, the water, and each other. These were clear, enduring moments we shared on the Cape, moments my mother would have liked.

The program assembled nightly in the lounge to tell stories. One night, our travel guide delivered his rendition of "Little Red Riding Hood," where the wolf was caught fornicating with the rotund grandmother instead of eating her. He made this recitation in the costume of the grandmother. Midway through the telling, he could barely keep in place the pillows escaping from under his shirt, pillows jarred loose by all the heavy laughter. Our travel guide said that laughter and the body couldn't be more connected, that laughter was necessary in order to find intimacy. As he ended his story, he took off his cargo shorts and proceeded to undress completely. He took his scarf and threaded it about the bulk of his balls, tying the remainder around his penis. After thus encasing himself, our travel guide ran off and disappeared into the darkness of the dunes. I tried to imagine the purpose of this lesson. Then it occurred to me that he might be a person living in a state of suffocation. Like any man might feel if he found himself trapped on board a condemned plane hovering above endless water with no flotation device. A few hours passed before everyone realized he wasn't returning, at least not any time soon. We agreed to get a good night's rest, and start fresh and early the following morning. I called and left Jim a message about the experience. I shared with him what I believed to be the point of the lesson. Isolation, I said to him on the machine, it does something maddening to an otherwise stable mind.

The next morning over breakfast in the dining hall, Margie, addressing the program, suggested we adjust to our travel guide's disappearance and get back to work. His absence would admittedly be an inconvenience, as he was our travel guide. The alternative was to leave early and go home, which received hostile rejection. Eventually the program decided it would be best to continue building our vernaculars, assuming any day now our travel guide would return. Group C piped up, confessing their eagerness to divulge the details of their experiment. On that note the program dispersed and re-gathered in the meeting room.

Group C presented their findings:

"Group C has come up with the concept of inherited memory. We conceived the idea while conducting a series of tests on the fish in the formidable aquarium on display in the hotel's lobby. One by one, members of Group C inserted into the tank a different but commonplace object: pen, screw, or twig. Each foreign object repelled the fish in the same manner. When an object was inserted into the fish tank, the fish would 'cower' at the bottom, clearly in avoidance of the object. Or perhaps the fish were recoiling in anticipation? Group C posits that the uniform response indicates, even if symbolically, that these fish, despite their genetic differences, have inherited the same information. Leading us to conclude that knowledge is accessed from what we term the inherited memory: it could be any kind of information, like a sense, bloodline, or landmark. According to Group C, 'inherited memory' is the source of all common memory, stemming from the histories we inherited, accessible to those continuing to survive. Histories, when tapped into, cause a uniform reaction. Like the fish," Group C said.

I looked around the room and saw myself as one woman among forty women who had chosen this very same adventure, for the sake of desire, and I was nodding in the very same way.

Announced over the loudspeaker was the news that our travel guide had been discovered nearby in the dunes, asleep under a tree, naked and severely sunburned. He had been healing for a few hours now, but he wouldn't be able to return and direct the remainder of our program, and therefore the program would be ending early. There would still be a final party set to take place in a few days, to wrap things up and send us off to our respective homes. Our partial refunds were waiting in envelopes at the front desk. The voice then apologized for the early dispatch and for any confusion the news might have caused.

On the advice of the other ladies, I gave up calling Jim. He also gave up, and the feeling in my bones wasn't hollow or ghostly at all. I became aware of this sensation one morning while walking along the shore by the hotel. I hadn't even noticed the absence of pain, of loss that I should have been feeling. My heart sank a bit, and I was puzzled, as if the life that had existed prior to this experience had been entirely unnecessary. But my mind was eager. Margie was by my side and the day was perfect. The gulls, as we began calling them, flew around in the sky as if surrounding a carcass. Everything was abundantly alive. The air smelled rich, like sun, fish, and sand. I couldn't have borne a smell of another kind.

On the day of our premature departure from the program, I wrote Jim a letter. It had been a few days since I'd heard any word and it seemed only fair to share with him my decision to remain. It was clear that I desired the salty atmosphere and that this was a good way to end. If all that was good were to remain, I would need to say goodbye. I wrote that I imagined him happy when I pictured him now; that I hoped he would find space in his heart to forgive us for failing so miserably at this union.

The final party took place over brunch. It was a lavish and fully catered affair that included fresh fruit, pamphlets, bite-sized tuna sandwiches, a whole branzino, and seltzer water in an abundance of natural flavors. Following lunch, and in the spirit of our travel guide, a fellow participant passed out fortune cookies. Margie read me the fortune from my cookie, as I was reluctant to unravel it myself. It read: "Life, it's all carrot and no stick!" We laughed hysterically, but stopped when a fellow visitor went up to take the stand and address the program. I placed a boning knife in my purse in recognition of what was to come. And as our fellow comrade was about to recount the story of a wolf that had made love to a rotund lady, I excused myself and walked out to the bay.

Fork

I felt sick. Somewhere between slicing your finger on the top of a can of crushed tomatoes and my cousins being sick bitches. It wasn't dirty, as a set of words or a personal composition. For the last few days, I've been wearing an oversized orange sweater. It hasn't been particularly chilly. The oversized sweater was "in" this season. I knew since I've been passing my time in the shopping mall, taking notes. There, I watched culture happen. I watched people make themselves through their fashion, through their purchases, and their chosen headspaces. I observed as they shaped their nature. In collections, in flocks like ducks, they moved seamlessly about the architecture—large bags, puffed and displayed, that served as flotation devices, cellphones attached like leeches to fingers, or screens alight with images of other faces to their faces. In the mall, people had purpose. They looked informed. I wanted that look.

A friend of mine who worked airport control was able to get me a last-minute deal on a flight to Providence. He asked what the ticket was for, and why the rush. I simply reminded him of all the past favors I've done him—walking his dog, loaning him money, making him soup when he was ill. I did these things and never questioned why he failed to call when he had a girlfriend. My mother had ingrained in me that when you give you should not expect to receive; otherwise, it's ransom. Eventually, he backed off. *I'm just concerned*, his text message read. *Just do this*, I wrote back.

Multiple department stores stocked the oversized sweater, cleverly (or not) referred to as the "Boyfriend Sweater." It was hard to decide between them. In the end, I settled on an orange one with light and dark vertical orange stripes. If I wasn't mistaken, a look-alike of someone famous recently wore something similar, and for a brief moment a number of notable shops ran out of stock. Vertical stripes were more flattering on the body, everyone who knows a good decision from a bad one says so, although that wasn't my issue. The bulky illusion of horizontal stripes could've added just the right amount of feminine curve to my gangly, slender figure. That would have been a more desirable outcome, but I wasn't in the mood to reward myself.

The sales clerk looked surprised when I brought the orange sweater up to the cash register.

"What about the other sweaters I brought in?" she protested. "I thought we agreed orange isn't your color…"

I gave her an inadequate smile. An adequate response would have been one that offered some consolation, a gesture that would make my temporary companion see that I hadn't left her out on purpose. I liked the sales clerk fine, but I really had other pressing relationships to attend to. Truth was, I had found the sweater on my own in the far back of the dressing rooms. It was on a rack along with the other disqualified clothing items. It, too, was hanging crookedly but fared better than the other items, those that had fallen from their hangers and lay crumpled on the floor.

"It has a giant hole under the armpit!" she said, pointing at the nickel-sized hole, her flexed finger determined to make me see my error.

"And look here!" she said, exasperated, her face spiraling inward like a Slurpee swirl. "Underneath this one too!"

I handed the sales clerk my credit card. She stuffed the orange sweater in a shopping bag. It had been years since I had last made a mall purchase, but I noticed that the sales clerk hadn't folded it nicely before bagging it. A formality I had previously understood to be mandatory. I nodded warmly to thank her and put on my sweater, leaving the bag on the counter. With new earrings, a fresh fork drawing on my hip, and my new orange sweater, I felt ready to go.

I haven't taken these pieces off since purchasing them. I wore them on my way to the airport. In my youth, I never would have behaved that way. I never would have worn the same items of clothing consecutively—what if someone spotted me? But it was the early 1990s then and nobody liked being misconstrued. Girls wore Guess jeans and wanted to be seen in a light and sexy way, but nobody wished to be called a "ho," or to catch chlamydia. Today, girls dressed like their boyfriends, casually and loosely, and pretended that their boyfriends found the idea attractive. My male students said it would be sexier if their girlfriends just borrowed their clothes instead, because that implies something. Giggle. I didn't waste my time asking what.

I reached my flight in time. Providence made an impression—you don't forget the details. It was damp. There were hot wieners. The mayor was re-elected from prison, and when he decided to eat a hot wiener, he rode a white horse downtown to get it. Perhaps Providence was significant because I won second place in a Whole Foods' Memorable Story competition. If I could write the story over, I would add a seeing-eye dog, or write about giving birth in the bulk section, especially near those energy nubs that tasted like they sounded. Those stories always win first prize. I wrote about finding love in the cheese aisle.

The passenger seated next to me constantly fidgeted with his keys. Earlier, he flossed his teeth. I read an article about how more and more people view airplanes as extensions of their personal space. More and more people are taking off their shoes and socks, not only for international flights, but also for domestic ones such as this. I didn't have a giant opinion on the matter, except I did believe for the most part that people should mind their own business. This has become harder to do now that people exposed openly, without provocation, their feelings, whether online or on t-shirts. And from what I've read, a vast number of Americans are currently at work on autobiographies.

For the past several days, after the mall closed, I would go home and undress myself. I'd prop the full-length mirror I received in junior high, cardboard frame intact, against the wall. Because of the way the mirror leaned, some parts of my body were ill-proportioned. At times it was frustrating. In the mirror, I studied myself with my new earrings on, and with my new red fork "tattoo," as if I were preparing to paint a self-portrait. If my mother knew about the fork drawing on my pelvis she'd have a hundred questions. Even if I told her it was just a drawing, she'd look askance. And if my mother knew about my new earrings, she'd say, "They're not even sterling!" My mother has a collection of sterling silver spoons that hung on some sort of sterling silver spoon contraption. One day those sterling silver spoons will belong to me. My mother reminded me of my inheritance—"what will one day belong to me"—especially when the holidays were near, when the two of us sorted through the delicates, when we unraveled and arranged the stowed-away plates and serving trays, revealing a collection of shiny matching objects. As was custom, we'd deliberately set the table. It was important we do this. This act that we performed around the table was significant because it's happened before. This act has occurred and will continue to occur, and the existence of it happening was in part connected to my presence, but its existence wasn't contingent on my presence.

The passenger next to me has been gone for some time. He must be peeing or stretching his legs. I'd read numerous articles about how important it was to do small exercises when you travel in order to keep up your circulation. Most airline magazines had illustrations in the back of them to remind passengers. Those tips have proven useful. I grew antsy when one of my body parts fell asleep. I was dressed as the professionals advised. My clothing wasn't constrictive, I made sure of it. I should've been more diligent about hydration, but there's nothing like boozing on an airplane, and I was taking a break from certain expectations.

The pilot announced our initial descent. The funeral was at 4 o'clock. I hadn't personally been invited to his funeral, but I will make it just in time. I might even be a little early. I'll need to be discreet; my striped orange sweater—not very discreet. "So it goes," my mother would say, and in recent years the sentiment has grown more fulfilling.

Mourning for me was inert. At first, the feeling—a mass of pictures, ideas, memories, and words—settled inside of my throat like clay lining. The feeling gathered in every crevice, and every valve and inlet filled and hardened. It sat there denser than mud, thick as sea fog mooring ships to the bay. It festered. It burrowed, so deeply I had no words. I saw no way out until I stumbled on his baby fork inside an H.P. Lovecraft novel. I had used it as a bookmark. It had his initials on it. At the time, we found the entire notion of a baby receiving a fork, especially a tiny one with initials on it, preposterous. Mimicking baby faces, like we imagined British entertainers might, we took turns miming tiny baby foods, with the tiny silver fork, into our teeny tiny baby mouths.

I retrieved the fork. I went to the kitchen. I took a trusty red pen and marked a thin medium-sized oval shape to target; I had one shot, red pens are tough to erase. I took the fork to my skin to measure, to align the tines of the fork to that of my flesh, and drew out the contours of the fork accordingly. The fork shape was just above my pelvis. It angled downward toward my feet. It was drawn this way to ensure it wouldn't trouble anyone. I would hate for the image to make a person suspicious. I'd hate for someone to think I'd actually hurt myself. When the fork drawing was complete, I set about my day. I checked email. I sent my mother a text message about the copy of Ovid's *Metamorphoses* I forgot to mention I borrowed. I wrote to my students, giving them an additional research day. "Wow! Thanks!" some wrote back, mostly the bad ones.

The passenger next to me returned. He seemed reluctant to do so but the flight attendants made sure he was seated and buckled tight as the plane made its slow descent. "Are you OK?" he kept asking me.

I suspected I looked gloomy, but I hadn't cried, not one tear since his death. But the passenger, he too looked at me like the sales clerk looked at me as she rumpled up the sweater and tossed it in a bag. He looked at me like the mailman did yesterday, noting, as I retrieved my bills, "We could really use the sun to come out, a little vitamin D is good for the spirits!" Like the taxi driver had, "You sure you want the airport?" It's uncommon to flag down taxis outside of New York City, and even more to hand the cabbie a piece of paper spelling out your destination. Or, like the ever-busier flight attendants, who'd been staring at me since boarding, long before reading my scribbled request for whiskey on a napkin, "Whiskey? I'm certain we've run out of it." And when I fiercely scratched out "whiskey" and wrote "VODKA," they pretended not to understand. I gave them some sort of look because eventually they handed me a drink.

I felt light-headed. No longer was I much of a drinker. Vodka had such terrible connotations for females. In college, I tried to distinguish myself. Instead of taking Jell-O shots and welcoming panty raids with high-pitched jubilance, I drank whatever I wanted and with assuredness avoided diet sodas. I lived off of eating hearty burritos—lots of rice with lots of whatever else was cheapest, mostly cilantro. I drank whiskey with him. He noticed me because, as he said, "you ate food." Our time was spent fucking, playwriting, and assembling a dish he fittingly called "beans," made of canned refried beans and hot sauce. Any can of beans and any bottle of hot sauce would do.

The plane landed. Because I hadn't packed anything other than a Band-Aid and the Lovecraft novel, I didn't need to wait for baggage claim, something I never liked doing, especially when I smoked. I might have been happier as a smoker, but once you know the truth it's hard to ignore. And then with the posting of images of sick babies and breathing-starved asthmatic patients on cigarette packs, all the imagination went away. He never smoked. He found it distracting.

Providence was overcast and forty-three degrees. I was snug in my sweater. My earrings held up. I handed the taxi driver the cemetery address. He turned up the radio. I felt shy on the way to the funeral I wasn't invited to attend, but read about on Facebook. On Facebook, everyone knew how to grieve. People posted warm messages of hope in the form of flowers or happy-faced emoticons. I deleted my account.

The taxi driver turned his head and asked if I would like to take a longer route. I nodded vertically. We passed by the Vietnamese restaurant where we occasionally met to catch up. Back then he would ask about my graduate school studies, I would ask about his new play, and he'd order a dish I could have a bite of. He could be generous that way. I remembered when my mother uneasily told me that she had not felt "he was the right person." I asked her why she waited to mention her feelings until long after we'd broken up. My mother said she felt it wasn't her place. She said she knew I'd figure it out on my own. "That's not the point," I distinctly remember telling her.

I saw the pictures. He died surrounded by family and friends, some of them ours, that we made together, and some I'll never know. There was a photograph with his new wife; I liked her, I could tell from the photo. I, too, would have preferred to say goodbye in person. To explicitly tell him I loved him. I never wrote out the words as precisely. Maybe I wrote them exactly, but "I love you" by itself rings deficient. Then again nothing can be known for certain because all communication between us had been done over email and email was without intonation. I knew I'd written, "Can I do anything?" "How can I help?" "I am thinking of you." "I am sending good thoughts." What a waste of words, though I meant every one of them.

I arrived early to the cemetery. I was alone except for a young boy and his mother laying out roses on a patch of perfectly articulated grass. They were clasping hands loosely. And as he would have wanted, I took out my book and picked up where I left off. The clouds moved. The sky darkened. A few pages in, I crawled inside of my gut and out through my eyes, but these things were not possible.

I felt lightheaded. I pulled up my orange sweater to peek at the red fork drawing. It was there. I began to howl and laugh ferociously. I grieved myself into an imperfect circle on the damp grass. The boy and his mother were briskly heading in my direction. Clutching the book in one hand, and his baby fork in the other, I rolled onto my back and looked at the sky. I thought about the Band-Aids tucked safely in my backpack.

The boy and his mother were close. I could smell them. They smelled sweet and kind and like a good omen. I wished to tell the mother and child about my own childhood. To share with them a bit about this goldfish named Pepper, that in the end had lived a very long life. Initially, my mother warned me that Pepper would not last through the night—the fish was used to being on display and traveling throughout America, seeing the sights. I told her that I would keep the fish in fresh water. I would love the fish. That's all it would take for it to prosper. I would put Pepper in a sturdy glass bowl with clean water and talk to it, lovingly, which calmed my mother and probably saved the fish's life.

That goldfish had outlived my mother's expectations. She had said Pepper would last a year. Three, tops. He lived for forty-two years, just shy of Tish—the oldest goldfish—who held the Guinness Book of World Records for the longest living goldfish in the world. I had won my nearly legendary, almost-champ fish at a state fair by clownishly throwing a dart at the ceiling, which in turn popped every target balloon on its way down to the ground. Kids with darts, fish, books—these things should not be underestimated. At the fair, those waiting in line to get their shot at winning applauded. It was unbelievable, they said, clapping, on their tippytoes to catch a view of the fish in its little baggy. This went on for a solid five minutes before they moved on to something else.

Distrito Federal

If Conlon wasn't busy composing music for the player piano, he spent his time mulling over cryptic scenarios that provoked his interest; for instance, how a boat constructed out of paper illustrated to resemble wood, looks like a boat constructed out of wood. He assembled this example. He made one wooden boat and one boat made from material approximating the look of wood. He photographed the two boats and asked their dinner guests to identify which one of them was real. He contended that both were indeed real but that only one was made of actual wood. His wife, Maria, laughed. Everyone else wiped their mouths. "No lo entiendo," Maria's closest friend, Lupe, said. Lupe asked her again why she had married a man that loved the mechanical piano. She asked, "How can he understand pleasure, when he's so preoccupied with structure?"

Home from her Monday outing, Maria undressed and stepped into the steaming bathtub in their attic. She cleaned herself. She hummed one of Conlon's new compositions. Maria washed herself not with cloth, but with paper. She had her reasons; she had her own kind of understanding. As she bathed, her body was situated between the bath water and the exposed electrical wire on the wall. It felt right to her. It just did. A very precarious position indeed, but so is being married to a Communist! she thought. Maria was inclined to think of the tub as something beyond its functional use. "For a woman to bathe properly, she should be naked. And this is a loaded stipulation," she once told Lupe. From the tub, Maria could see framed duplicates of Manet's *Le déjeuner sur l'herbe* and Ingres' *La Grande Odalisque* hanging on the wall.

Maria sat back in the tub. Abrupt vibrations from below interrupted her thinking. She quickly retrieved herself. She considered fear. Conlon was a quiet, deliberate man, not to mention

Conlon was on his way to the grocery. Instead, she put on her robe and walked downstairs. On the first floor was an unknown man with large hands, standing in their corridor. He smoked Soberbios; he did not smoke Delicados, as Conlon did. He was holding a rifle. "Just to show you that I know how to use it," he assured her. Maria read his lips shape those words, and was not impressed. But she was not entirely alarmed; these sorts of occurrences happened in Mexico. She studied the man's mouth closely.

"You are dripping," the man said. Maria moved toward him. It jarred him. He stepped back and caught himself in the oval mirror hanging on the wall. He jolted in surprise. Something about his reflection alarmed him. His rifle fell to the linoleum floor. Maria swiftly picked up the rifle. She tightened the belt of her robe and backed up.

"The weight of so much death," she explained, looking at the rifle in her slim hands. The man standing before her seemed amused. He regained his composure. Maria felt the rifle. "When I touch this object," she said, "I know that I am to grasp it tightly with both hands. Just like this," she showed the man.

"I'm impressed," he said. He was not nervous.

"The gestures are like childbirth," she explained to the stranger. "The *how to* is inherited, it's nothing one learns, it's automatic." Maria then aimed the rifle at the unknown man. "I place my finger on the lever and pull hard. After this action, a precise and recognizable sound and scene will occur. At that time, I should feel differently about you being here in our house," Maria said.

With the rifle steady in her hands, Maria approached the unknown man and performed the graphic described: she aimed and fired. The pressure produced a volcanic impact on the man's chest. She watched him feel for the hole, reaching to extinguish the bullet that had lodged itself deeply. He naturally and frantically gripped the bloody dent until he was grip-less. He fell to the linoleum. Maria scrutinized the once-standing man, who was now lying on the floor, silent and bleeding, but instead of seeing a human body, she saw an image of a turkey. An inedible turkey was what Maria saw. She couldn't shake it. At first this amused her, but then immediately she felt guilty. Any dead man is a shame, she thought. Better leave the scene for Conlon to figure out, Maria decided. Maria relaxed. Conlon will understand the burden of such a threat, she thought, as she went outside to wake up. Outside, seeking air, their neighborhood of San Angel was too quiet for a Monday afternoon. The air was unusually still. The sky was sunless. She wondered why the vista never changed. She wasn't spent by it, but it never changed.

Conlon returned home from the grocery to find the neighbors in their corridor, surrounding the dead man on the linoleum floor. They'd heard the shot and had come over. They'd waited longer than they would have liked before deciding it was crucial to check on the scene. They didn't want to seem intrusive, and they didn't want to get hurt themselves. The door was unlocked. The neighbors promised they knocked first before entering. They told Conlon they recognized the fallen man, noting his large hands looked familiar. Some said he was a drug addict, some said he was a corrupt cop. Some said he was a drifter. Another convinced some others that the fallen man was Maria's father, who had reluctantly returned from the dead to do as Maria's mother had all her life instructed that he do more forcefully, which was to teach her lessons on why not to be alone.

Conlon lit another cigarette. Lupe had stopped by; she wondered openly where Conlon had been. Conlon lifted the brown bags full of groceries. An apple fell to the floor. The neighbors dispersed. The police came and took care of business quickly and without confrontation. The body was hauled off in a sheet. Lupe insisted on cleaning up the disorder. Conlon went to find Maria. She was in the backyard. With Lupe's help, Conlon took Maria to bed. Conlon moved their heavy old cat aside and opened their bedroom window. Maria quickly fell asleep. Shortly thereafter, Conlon fell asleep next to her on her side of the bed. Lupe finished cleaning up the mess. She then closed and locked the front door behind her.

Panel Vs. Board

Lucretia was finally on a panel. She couldn't resist the impulse to get out to Los Angeles. The topics to be covered at the conference included all things related to women, gender, and the importance of the novella. She was planning to write more on these topics and had been invited by a friend, another female writer, who also had published novellas with small presses. Both Lucretia and her friend had well-established husbands who had published volumes of novels with big-time publishers. Both women lived in New York, but Lucretia and her husband were the only couple to remain in Manhattan. They had no children, a bit of a sore point between them, a topic that had come up before at one of her rare readings: what did she know about children? She did explain to them that she was a fiction writer and therefore capable of research and imagination. She said she had also been a child once, if that made any difference. It never escaped her to feel bemused that her husband, the well-known novelist, had written extensively about children in his books. But no one ever questioned him.

Lucretia and her husband had a two-story walk-up on MacDougal, across the street from Patti Smith, whom they knew on a first name basis. Many of their acquaintances, including Patti, didn't know that in addition to her husband, Lucretia was a writer. The subject of her also being a writer had come up at one of their dinner parties. Lucretia had again published a novella with a small press and her husband was openly commending her talent. "My wife, the talent!" were the words he chose to express himself. This, of course, prompted a larger conversation, many asking Lucretia what it was exactly she had done. She had written another small novel, she told them. Since her editor, whom she felt entirely grateful to have, suggested she stay brief in her ambition, she kept this detail to herself. Her latest novella, entitled *Panel vs. Board*, was about two boxers that always tied. It wasn't satire exactly, it wasn't metaphor either, she explained. "It's just a small story," she said to those asking. Her husband beamed, as he always did, when she'd open up a little about herself.

Lucretia had received many invitations to attend panels and to join boards, all of which, until very recently, she had coolly declined. She couldn't commit to two words that in nearly every respect were the same. They both could mean a separate or distinct part of a surface, something she felt she could connect to, since she too felt like a part of a surface.

When she arrived in Los Angeles, the weather was not what had been advertised on the plane. It was sunny and bright, and she noticed this was reassuring to all those visitors coming in from out of town. The pilot had suggested there would be light drizzle. On her hour drive into downtown from the airport, several meteorologists on the radio suggested a chance of drizzle. Perhaps through the evening. Maybe blistering heat all day. No one felt the need to commit to any particular type of weather. Los Angeles was vast, with inland areas, mountains, valleys, and coastal regions. How could anyone be expected to know for certain?

The young man working the mini-store in the lobby of the downtown hotel where the conference was being held ran out of sunglasses in less than an hour.

"After all, you're in Los Angeles," he explained to her, "and it's hard to avoid the desire to feel discreet in Los Angeles."

"I thought the desire was to avoid wrinkles forming around the eyes."

He offered Lucretia his extra pair, pulling the shades from an army bag, saying they belonged to his predecessor who had left the job and returned to Colorado, where he claimed the air was fresher.

"And thinner and drier," she added.

The young man had never been out of Southern California, and as he said, he couldn't see any reason to. The young man explained to Lucretia that if she wasn't fond of the extra pair, she could surely locate some in the "lost and found" department. She took the neon plastic sunglasses and thanked the young man.

Outside, the sun was blasting, the heat more than she could bear. It wasn't as though summers in New York weren't swelteringly painful, it was more that in Los Angeles the expectation was to be better than, or distinct from, your previous self. All this to say, that in a place like Los Angeles, Lucretia felt she needed to look well-maintained at all times, like Joan Didion had looked all those years she'd lived there.

Young girls with sun-bleached locks skated by on rollerblades.

"They're tourists," the young man from the mini-store pointed out as he lit a cigarette. He told her people don't rollerblade downtown and that people moving to Los Angeles from the Midwest, or Colorado, generally looked more Californian than Californians.

"What about people from New York?"

"Oh, those people don't visit at all, and if they do, they bitch and moan the whole time," he answered.

She asked the young man for a cigarette and offered him a five-dollar bill, since she felt rude taking again something for free from someone as young as he was. She had her own pack but that wasn't the point. He refused the bill and Lucretia lit up.

The taste of tobacco made her horny; she thought about her days in graduate school. She would sit at her desk that looked out onto a hospital parking lot and write. Her husband, then her skinny boyfriend, would snuggle up to her, kissing her ears, wrapping his tongue around her lobe. He would do this to her lobes and she would picture small pigs in a blanket and think about how as a child she was forbidden to eat such things. Her then-boyfriend would traipse about their small apartment in Providence, naked and consistently erect. He told her that watching her work was too arousing: "I can't concentrate, and how about a break to nibble?" Lucretia thought about when they married, it was she, and not he, who was expected to be the more successful one. She wasn't sure what had happened despite the piles of self-help books her mother insisted she read. She read a few, but in the end, they were all the same: she was burdening herself and she should work hard to unburden herself.

It was not as though Lucretia was unhappy, she had just found herself in a place so familiar, a place she had read about numerous times before, that it made her ill. As a result, she dismantled her smartphone and took up smoking. She refused to offer an explanation to her bewildered husband, who now was pounds heavier and roamed about their home in a terrycloth robe. She no longer debated the subtle suggestion of font types, or whether prosecco was worth the cost, or whether one should just hold out for champagne. In fact, she would admit publicly that she loved Italy more than France, but she knew it would create a social mess. It wasn't that Lucretia felt she was being detained from her own life, or the things she aimed to create, she just felt that the Great American Novel had already been defined and she had not been included in its definition. There wasn't any room for her in the way there was room for great writers such as her husband. She felt catty and searched her bag for a cigarette. Essays, personal and otherwise, novellas, and short stories, these were the forms most available to her, and there was nothing inherently wrong with that. She could even dabble in song and poetry, if she felt obliged. She did feel lucky.

Lucretia lit a cigarette only to put it out immediately. She knew she could do something about it, join a women's club or spend all night on TikTok, obeying new friends famous for seeing and therefore understanding their followers, but she wasn't compelled to participate in that discourse. It made her uneasy. She remained unconvinced. A perpetual non-believer. She wasn't one to complain, and when she'd say that to her mother, her mother would retort, "It's not complaining, Lucretia, it's getting what you want."

She continued her novella writing. She had come to understand one advantageous aspect of small presses: they didn't mind her nonlinear, untraditional approach to writing. And despite the fact that she didn't like being pigeonholed as "nonlinear" and "untraditional," she increasingly didn't mind going unnoticed. When she viewed her husband's career, she saw a gregarious monster of an ego, she saw a man who wrote to be noticed. Others viewed her husband's career as forthright and lovable. Both men and women found him wildly charming but safely docile. Women felt he understood their inner selves, and men congratulated him. His readers were grateful he could produce sympathetic male characters while keeping female readers satisfied. Her husband was known notoriously for being easygoing and undyingly, even emotionally, erudite. He was engaging even to those who didn't read; he didn't step on anyone's toes. Lucretia admired his undoubted commitment to himself. She should be willing to say things about herself, open herself up to the world, and let the world inside. At the very least, open herself up to their immediate literary community, as her husband had requested many times. Her agent had advised her it would be helpful to her career. Her agent, along with her mother, had suggested Lucretia make use of her commanding presence and attractive gait. She lit another cigarette and smoked it down to the butt, inhaling the last drag deeply. She forgot about exhaling, and in her flurry, she no longer found the Los Angeles heat oppressive.

Lucretia woke up at 5 p.m., her mouth tasting of tobacco and whiskey. The young man from the mini-mart in the lobby was in bed next to her. His cotton V-neck still on his fit but small body. She had taken him back to her room, had given him head and then they had fallen asleep. The hotel phone rang and the young man jolted awake.

"The flight was easy, up and then down," she said into the receiver. And, "Don't forget the plants in the spare room."

The young man was now up, putting on his trousers, lighting a cigarette. Lucretia waved to him to open the doors that led out onto a large patio overlooking a marble-blue pool. She stood up unabashedly, her thin but toned body there to be seen in the barely dimming natural light. He looked in at her from the balcony, the gape in his mouth large enough to lose his cigarette. He removed it before it had the chance to fall out, and made it obvious he was ready for her. She said goodbye and hung up the phone.

The conference began at 7 a.m. Lucretia had met the friend who'd invited her at the café in the lobby. They had coffee and refrained from embracing the displayed buffet items. They would soon be entering a conference room the size of the Titanic, brimming with muffins, cakes, danishes, bagels, and butter. There were people starving in downtown Los Angeles, and in any given year residents feel it's the worst yet. Her friend asked how she'd slept and commented on how well Lucretia looked after a long day of travel. While scarfing danishes, they talked about sugar decaying not only your teeth but your insides, the weather back home in New York, and the topics included in the conference. She asked Lucretia if she would be willing to discuss what it was like to be married to a famous author because they—the organizers of the event—had thought it would be of interest to the majority of guests.

"You know," she said, "people just want to know what it's like to be married to someone so talented."

Lucretia nodded diagonally, and bit at her thumbnail. She could still smell the young man. Sugar was good for her; she determined she would become the exception to the rule.

"You know, Lucretia, people are very interested in the fact that you're both writers, married, living in New York City, and childless. It's a rare breed these days since children are as popular as buying organic," her friend went on.

Lucretia scolded herself for accepting the invitation. She'd been wary that this conference, like the others, would request that she discuss her husband's first novel. It was his breakthrough. It sold more copies than *The Catcher in the Rye* and had ricocheted him into the highest of literary stratospheres. It was a Great American Novel about Lucretia and about their life together. He had not told her that all of the things she'd confided in him would one day make the page. He had not told her he'd borrowed her words both written and oral in order to cast a clear and honest picture, "a raw and very human ambiguity" that would become the hallmark of his work. He had not told her she wouldn't be credited as co-author because, as he explained, "writers don't really do that sort of thing." She had never spoken publicly about the book, not even when he implored her to, or to at the very least speak to its gravitas at the book launch. Here she was in Los Angeles, caught like a fish on a line.

"Yes," she said under her breath, "caught in something as generic of a phrase as that one." Realizing she had uttered the sentiment aloud, she lit the cigarette that had been stored behind her ear, something she'd noticed the young man do.

"Lucretia, this café is non-smoking. In fact, you can't smoke inside anywhere. It's the same as in New York," her friend told her.

"Guess I better take it outside then," Lucretia said, as she stood up.

Lucretia sat down with the other panelists at five to seven. They had reiterated over the loudspeaker how essential it was to begin the process on time. The trays passed from panelist to panelist were overflowing with pastries and bite-sized sandwiches. "Would you like a slider?" another panelist offered. She nodded and stuffed a few bite-sized sandwiches in her bag to give the young man, who had appeared to her to be underfed. She had watched his ribs all night as he breathed; with each breath nothing inflated. In the morning, she had asked him if he was hungry. He had nothing to lose in this life but one mutt, nothing to care for other than the dog he called Hard Wired. Lucretia had a pet once, a guppy in a bowl that lived in their kitchen. They'd only had it a short while before it leapt out of the bowl and onto the counter. It took her a few days to notice it there. Her husband had been away, promoting his new book across Europe. Eventually, she sealed the dead guppy in a sandwich bag and stored it in the freezer, hoping to one day give it a proper burial. It was only then, in the morning and after the long night with a man who she learned had a pup named Hard Wired, that she remembered the guppy was there.

The conference began. It was rough at first since they couldn't get the overhead projector to work and the hotel receptionist kept running back and forth in her tight skirt and wobbly heels until she finally burst out into tears, "This is not my job!" At least one person in the audience applauded her, or so Lucretia thought, before the images of transgendered, multi-racial female couples with their families showed up on the screen, wedged between the pages of a thin book. The title: *The Novella: Women, Gender, and the Page.* Each panelist introduced those to the left of them. Lucretia had not been prepared but managed to get something out of her mouth that resembled an informative compliment. After introductions, they rattled through matters such as the role of childbirth as fodder for female writers (Lucretia kept her mouth locked shut), to elementary principles of writing, notably concision (she kept her comments brief). The panelists failed to discuss the novella, and she didn't remind them.

What was it that made breasts so uncomfortable not only for the woman who has them but also for the men who look at them? Lucretia thought, when the panelist next to her finished explaining the plight of the good American novel. If she exposed a breast right then and there, it would make everyone in the room uncomfortable, despite the fact they'd all at one point in their existence had one in their mouths. As another panelist wrapped up her comments, noting the group had digressed and in doing so had failed to address the importance of the novella—she had in fact said "impotence," which set the crowd alight with laughter.

"Regarding the evolution of the novella, let me just say novellas are no less a novel than their fellow counterparts," the panelist said, closing out.

Lucretia thought about how the baby kitten she'd rescued had turned out to be pregnant at the same time the Dominique Strauss-Kahn saga began, the saga that included a hotel maid. In 2011, Will and Kate married, and Congresswoman Gabrielle Giffords was shot in the head. It was the same year Osama bin Laden was killed. It was a big year, it was the year her husband won another prestigious award, and in the crowded and decorated room, he had in his acceptance speech dedicated it to her.

"This one's for Lucretia Williams," said a young woman with big black sunglasses on. It was bright in the conference room. There were many skylights and windows, so Lucretia didn't think twice about it. But she did wonder where her shades had gone. Had she misplaced them?

The young woman went on, "You've been married to Mr. Williams for many years. You met in college and he followed you to graduate school. Yet, you rarely speak about his work even though you too are a writer. You speak even less about your personal lives, even though all of his work seems devoted to it. Can you explain why now you are here, open to answering these questions? I do recognize mine is the first and perhaps the last..." this final part was muddled. Embarrassed, the young woman struggled to comfortably sit back down. The room went quiet. Lucretia fumbled around in her jacket for a lighter and began telling her, and all those present in the conference room, about her latest novella, the one about the two boxers that never won. Two boxers, one named Panel and one named Board, that always tied no matter how many bouts they fought. When she was asked to expand further, to get back to the question at hand, "What about Mr. Williams?" she took out a cigarette and said, "I am pretty sure I am not forgetting anything."

Her Cousin Lena

Rose kept a notebook near and recorded her phone conversations with her mother, just because. A part of her, the part that supported herself and paid for her condoms, cigarettes, and rent, assumed a recording of her conversations with her mother might one day come in handy. Her mother wasn't afraid of psychological blackmail. She was constantly reminding Rose of the things she should be grateful for. Rose was grateful. She pressed record.

Rose's mother's voice was muffled by wind sounds; she was driving along a busy highway in Southern California with her windows open. Just the sort of thing her mother would do in order to complicate the conversation, which in this case was about an advertisement Rose had placed in a newspaper. Rose wrote the advertisement as an experiment. Though, because nobody had yet responded, the outcome remained uncertain. The ad Rose placed requested *something* deranged. At first it had read *someone* deranged, but Rose quickly realized that wasn't quite right.

What does *something deranged* even mean? her mother demanded.

Rose explained to her mother, who was angling to get into a car accident (as was her way), that she had written the advertisement using those words because she imagined a response that would be more direct.

How's your thesis advisor? Rose's mother asked.

It was a big question, whether Rose's mother simply avoided taking the bait or if she simply didn't listen to a thing her daughter said. Rose bet on the former because, despite being a terrible driver who insisted on driving, her mother was not a stupid woman.

He's narrow and arguable, Rose answered her mother.

Rose's mother insisted on knowing if her daughter was subsisting on coffee produced from a plastic cone: What's wrong with electric coffeemakers? Why all the fuss about taste, about nuance? I'd be remiss not to point this out, her mother said, defiantly sucking and smacking on her nicotine gum.

Her mother then requested that Rose listen up and stop fucking around with experiments and get busy engaging with the public in a less abstract manner. Why not go to a mall? Or a movie?

Rose knew when to ignore her mother. She admired her mother, plotted to assassinate her mother, or ignored her mother. At her age, those were the remaining options.

The sound! It's all muffled! her mother complained, before quickly going on to ask Rose if she was spending the entirety of her days in the library.

Remember, Rose, you need fresh air, her mother reminded her. Ever since you were a little girl you needed air. Perhaps you should consider getting a small pet. Pets are calming.

Her mother saw so many young people Rose's age contently walking small dogs around in the middle of the day, like they had no place else to be. Her mother wouldn't even speculate about how they fed the creatures, given the job market. She wouldn't worry Rose about the future.

Give me a minute, her mother said, as she repositioned herself. Her car seat was sticky, she explained. It was sweaty and sunny and sticky in Southern California, and she'd spilled her diet iced tea all over her lap. It was the least they could know about one another.

Sure thing, Mom.

Rose tried her mother on her ten-minute work breaks. She smoked on her break and was looking forward to finishing her cigarette. Because after her cigarette, the call would be over and she would feverishly lick her menthol-flavored lips, up and down, down and up, like a high-speed elevator. She never carried mints or orange-flavored lozenges or even tea tree oil toothpicks to mask the smell. On her smoke breaks, Rose considered packing up her shit in

Brooklyn and moving farther west to Washington State or Alaska, although she knew that wouldn't get her anywhere. Alaska would one day be submerged in water. But people still did it. They moved west to discover something new.

Have you heard from your cousin Lena? her mother asked, for the hundredth time in the last week. She's so pretty and so lonely, her mother said about Rose's cousin Lena. To think how popular Lena once was.

For a moment, Rose considered hitting pause on the recording. She felt like a penguin that continues to flap its wings without ever getting off the ground.

I worry most about the popular ones, Rose's mother went on. If I recall correctly, her mother said, your cousin was pretty darn good at putting sentences together. She could help you with your advertisement. Lena knew how to grab attention, even if she's struggling now in her tiny studio apartment stuffed with feral cats. Rose's mother only wished her daughter would eat something nutritious. She only wished her daughter would forget about the silly ad.

Why print anyhow? her mother asked. I thought youth spent more time online? Aren't all the available men online?

But that had nothing to do with it. Jesus, what did men have to do with it?

Rose had in fact contacted her cousin Lena about the advertisement, and her cousin had suggested that Rose aim to get what she wanted by pretending. Her cousin advised Rose to imagine a language for water jugs. Lena said guys like fluidity. She suggested Rose try to be more relaxed in general. She said, *Rose, be tranquil. Think: turquoise. Think: Taos, New Mexico. Limitless landscape, limitless barren landscape, and you are the water jug.* Lena said water jugs and turquoise were the epitome of relaxed, and that Rose should endeavor to be that way.

I see, her mother said understandingly. Well, as long as you recognize that the simulation of drowning isn't really drowning.

Rose's mother had an uncanny knack at changing the subject matter when it suited her. Like the time when Rose nearly cut off her pointer finger and her mother returned home with a synthetic tangerine blouse from Sears, or when she told her mother she was gay and her mother gave her four Norco and two fingers of gin and sent her off to nap.

Humor me, Rose. Jesus, where's your sense of humor? You used to be funny! I bet your cousin Lena would have something to say about the importance of humor. I know she'd agree with me if I said fun and humor are good for a relationship's longevity.

Mom, is it off-putting that I want to be called a cunt in bed?

I need a real cigarette, her mother said. Your experiments are killing me, Rose. Go forward, you useless asshole, it's a green light! her mother yelled into the receiver.

Mom, did you try honking?

Rose's mother asked if she'd made her doctor's appointment for her IUD replacement. It was important to keep up on these things, her mother reminded her.

Mom, can I tell you something that's weighing on me? Rose asked, when she sensed an opening.

I'm trying to listen, Rose, I really am, her mother said.

Earlier that day, as Rose made her way to work, she'd come across a blindfolded child, and now it was all she could think about. It was hailing in Greenpoint. The boy was drenched to the bone, icy and alone in a fenced-in yard, relentlessly hitting a piñata in the shape of a donkey with a baseball bat. *Wack. Wack. Wack.* Over and over, like neither he, nor the piñata, nor the bat, were really there, like they were imitations of what life should be like.

Was he sick? Was it his birthday? her mother speculated.

Rose had stopped to ask the blindfolded child if he needed any help, and when she looked inside the affected paper donkey, it was empty. Not a single piece of candy or plastic toy was inside. The boy wasn't after candy or prizes or treats. He was unfazed by the emptiness of the donkey.

Perhaps he isn't bothered by anything, her mother said.

That's just it, Rose said. Perhaps he's bothered by everything.

I'm pulling into the driveway now, Rose's mother cautioned about the dwindling reception. That damned mangled rat is still on the barbed wire fence! she yelled into the receiver.

Rose wanted to be helpful. She despised herself for it, her tendency to be helpful when she should have been setting up boundaries to protect herself. Rose would try again tomorrow on her break.

Mom, you know you can use the rake to catapult the rat into the ravine for the hawks to fetch.

What's that? Listen, Rose, make sure to contact your cousin Lena. Be grateful that she loves you like a sister. I can't bear to think of her with all this weather, and to think of her all alone in that stuffy studio apartment, cats crawling over her furniture, crawling all over her pretty face during this time of year. You, I know you'll get by. You always do, Rose.

I think I'm losing you, Mom.

The moment came, that itchy moment in a call when you don't know if it has dropped, if your words are no longer being received. Rose's finger moved to stop recording, but she just let it hover there.

Owls Yawn, Too

It sounded at first like hollow knobs floating in a storm. As ridiculous as it was to her husband, and their then-teenage daughters, it was her first description. Her husband and her two daughters never heard a sound.

In the morning, before leaving for her job at the textile company, she'd put out a thread of inviting snacks. Would he be hungry? In the moonlit evenings, she waited. On nights when he visited, she was invigorated; it was primal. On nights he failed to appear, she roamed the overgrown yard in search of a sign, of some indication of his presence. What was the system? What was it that determined his showing up? Those nights without him, without his sounds, were spent outside waiting until the tired and cold overcame her. Then, however reluctantly, before dawn she'd return indoors, return to their bedroom, to their bed where her husband lay soundlessly asleep. She'd return to her side where the reading lamp remained lit.

She would rise before anyone else in the house and drive to her job in Glendale. She would park in the adjacent lot and lock by hand her '90s Champagne Corolla, a trunk filled with disposables left by their two daughters. Then she would make her way inside the concrete building where she struggled to stay alert to do her job after a night of no rest. The work routine was not unbearably predictable, as their youngest college-bound daughter had asserted, but reassuringly predictable, easy and maintainable, unlike their then-college-aged daughters. She took what she could get by way of simplicity.

Often the first to arrive, she would get the coffee machine going, turn on the overhead lights, and then the air conditioning. The windows did not open. She would pilfer the fridge, searching for treats that she could eat without getting caught by her co-workers, and then restock the shelf-stable coffee creamer on the counter. Her boss, Nurit, who would be second to make an appearance, preferred Nescafé and had suggested to her many times before that she need not take on the task of making drip coffee since nobody did anything in that place save for the three of them. But Connie, who was one of them, drank regular, and the older Armenian women in the back did also. Nurit agreed that the Armenian women in the back deserved more. Everyone in the building drank out of Styrofoam cups. Nurit's company, comprised of three employees, occupied a quarter of the unaffable building in Glendale. The building was shared with another, larger, textile company. Nurit's operation was smaller, just the three of them, and occasionally Jane, who as far as anyone knew came out of nowhere. The older Armenian women in the back belonged to the other company.

Connie was not much older than she was. When she began the position at Nurit's textile company, Connie had been the one to train her. The position didn't have a title. It was a nameless job. For those two weeks, they worked closely alongside each other. Connie told her how a doctor had dropped an operating tool in her body when he'd gone to tie her tubes. He'd left it there. After living with excruciating pain, she finally had it removed. Connie spent those two weeks of training preoccupied by the news of a woman's death in an Arizona airport. The dead woman was a stranger, but, as Connie explained while demonstrating how to properly cut fabric for samples, she was not unfamiliar. The woman had been on her way from New York to some small town in Arizona, to stay in what Connie described as a healing clinic. The woman had not taken her original direct flight to Phoenix. And by the time she arrived in Phoenix, she was late and had missed her other, shorter flight, which would have taken her to heal. The airport officials told her the flight had been overbooked and she would be put on the next one. The woman was depressed, and she told the officials she needed to make that flight. It was imperative, the woman explained to them, for her to be on that flight. And when they denied her, she grew, as one official told the authorities, "hysterical." This description provoked the steel ire in Connie. The woman in the airport was then handcuffed and dragged to a windowless room, where she was left and later found dead.

At noon on the nose, she would distribute bananas: one to Connie's cubicle, the second in charge; one to her boss, Nurit, who had the only realized office space. Nurit was an avid tennis player. She was tan, lean, and sporty, with ambitions that went beyond designing cubicle curtains. She was more of an artist, born in South Africa, Jewish, a world traveler. The final banana she gave to herself. She set the yellow fruit in the back with the rolls of fabric and the little radio she listened to the news on. Sometimes, she offered her banana to the Armenian women, not all of them and at one time of course, but they weren't interested. All that Nurit, Connie, and she ate (out of loyalty which had become a habit), was a single banana at noon. It was a starved ritual that united the three women in the textile company. Absurd, but like in ritual it served a purpose: it kept them connected in a place that suffered from distinct qualities of estrangement.

Connie smoked menthols and did the accounting and other secretarial work. She often did Connie's filing for her; such was dictated by her lower status in the company. The task of filing for Connie had a dual function: it served to remind her of her underprivileged status among them, person of third importance (unless Jane showed up). And it served to remind her that she was not Nurit's closest employee—that space was reserved for Connie.

She had helped Connie once. She had come through for Connie on a personal matter. Together, they had furiously driven through the night down to San Diego to unearth her dead cat. Connie had had a long-term boyfriend who had moved back in with his parents in San Diego after he had lost his job, and could no longer pay his half of the rent. In an act previously intended to indicate her commitment to their relationship, Connie had agreed to bury the cat in his parents' backyard for safekeeping, since inevitably they would be moving around a lot. The economy had not survived. Connie agreed to it, and she buried her dead cat in his parents' backyard. It would be something the two of them as a couple would have forever, even though her then-boyfriend never did a thing for that cat, even though he didn't even like his parents, even though she would one day hold a management position which would allow her to buy a small place of her own with her own plants to water in the ground. Then, abruptly, the boyfriend ended their relationship. He had met someone over the internet who lived in China, and was quick to depart. For years, Connie mourned and wrestled with her guilt, with her feelings of betrayal. She had loved her cat most of all. With shovels and a wicker basket lined with a silver linen cloth, she and Connie jumped the wire fence surrounding his parents' house and proceeded to try and locate the buried animal. Connie had sworn she'd left an American flag, one of those small ones that people wave at parades, to mark the spot. But looking over the property now, there were at least two dozen of those wavy flags peeking out from the soil. "Cluck this," Connie said. She said she wanted to swear, but that it was too early to admit defeat. By hole seven she was noticeably anxious. "Damn," she said, on discovering a golf ball. They had dug several more holes on the property, looking for a cadaver, before Connie mentioned that along with it was a wad of cash in a Minnie Mouse tin. Like a sizable amount of cash? A wad, Connie confirmed, thereby raising the stakes of the find.

They would not give up. They had driven all that way. Finally, they unearthed the bundle of plastic bags bandaging plastic bags, which contained the cat and the tin with a lot of cash. It can be exceptionally hard to explain how deeply relieving a moment like that can be—to come across what you've been seeking for years—but she wanted to try. She told Connie she felt bodiless, like a feather. Connie said that was fucking weird but that she could try harder to understand how that could be. Together, they drove back to Los Angeles with what they'd come for. On the drive, Connie said she would never again be anyone's sucker.

She liked her job at the textile company. Both Nurit's and the larger company, which occupied the majority of the building, and which for the most part remained separate entities, came together on occasion to share birthday cakes and songs. The other, much larger company, went to Dodger games for celebratory reasons: a promotion, an engagement, Christmas, and anniversaries. The employees in the larger company stored their food, like Greek yogurt and protein bars—the quality ones that needed to be refrigerated—in the fridge, and often forgot about it, which made consuming them simpler. Those belonging to the larger company maintained friendly appearances, engaged daily in regular company tasks: chatting college sports and gas prices, taking regular coffee and bathroom breaks, making some professional phone calls, and seamlessly accomplished nothing.

There was a radio in the back where her workstation was, where her banana sat at noon. On her feet, listening to the news, her day passed comfortably: cutting fabric, making samples, labeling, sorting, answering the phone, filling orders, faxing documents, making organizational improvements, conducting inventory maintenance, shipping, and receiving. She didn't need for much during those hours she spent at the company. In the windowless back room, in her designated corner, surrounded by rolls of fabric covered in plastic to protect them and labeled in her handwriting: Primrose, *Teal*; Primrose, *Sun*; Primrose, *Tan* (each style had three color options). From her place in the back, she could see the older Armenian women sew and grommet. And occasionally, when hands were low, she would join them. They looked at her as though she must have had something better to do; the entire reason they were there was so that their children wouldn't need to be. She took her job seriously. It baffled them. They never asked her directly, but it had been insinuated: Why was she still there? To her children, who had never stepped foot inside the building, she described the lighting as "Eastern Promises" after she and her eldest daughter, then a newly engaged fresh-faced attorney, had gone to see the movie together.

Perhaps it's hard to explain, but purpose—like her nameless position—did a lot to address her loneliness. She understood what was needed from her. Her workspace was clean, organized. Others cut the fabric unevenly. Wasteful, she would say. It would then need to be re-cut in order to provide an adequate sample, one depicting the entire pattern just as it would repeat across a full yard. Sending samples was vital since the picture that was used to represent the fabric was inadequate. Pictures never did a pattern justice. And if a person had no imagination, it was impossible to picture how the patterns would look in a hospital.

At dusk, outside on an Adirondack chair she had borrowed from Connie, in an attempt to emulate owl sounds, she would call out. Her dull calls were not the deep, resonant hollow knobs floating in a storm she'd heard him make. Her sounds were human. She felt lame.

On the dirt, she left him trails of daintier fare, such as tiny scorpions, mice, and frogs. If the opportunity presented itself, she might offer him her husband and two daughters. It disquieted those in her company, such as her family—the carrion was stinky and animal. "Frogs are tender and kind," their few friends who still came for dinner reasoned, hoping to dissuade her from forking them over. "This situation is a murky one; nobody else hears anything," these same friends, who diminished in number, protested.

She would nod, taking in their reasonable suggestions to back away from the owl to focus on the humans in her life, while going on to offer their guests seconds: charred meat from the grill and cold side salads. Sometimes, she would say to a table of their dwindling friends, that owls kill members of their own species, which made for even fewer dinner guests. After the house was quiet, after everyone had gone home and the dirty dishes had been dealt with, she persisted, laying out the dead snacks. She knew he was watching. His eyes didn't move in his sockets, but it didn't matter because he could swivel his head more than one hundred eighty degrees to look in any direction. They procreate by rubbing noses together and eating fresh prey, and then sticking it in.

Her daughters, now grown women with complete lives as mothers and pet owners, no longer teased her for being in love with the owl, who they maintained was not *really* there. Instead, they concluded that they found her behavior endearing, a word she cringed at hearing. It was worse than belittling. She had not been in love with the owl, as her triangulated family and few friends for years had testified; she had been besotted with the owl. A distinction she could not request that they understand. What would Connie have said? Where had Connie gone? The times she had tried to find her, knowing that she was out there, she had come up empty-handed. There were too many Connie Lopezes in Southern California, and though she tried calling each listing, one by one, she recognized that in her lifetime she would never be able to reach them all.

The Great Horned Owl was the most adaptable. The great owl could live for up to twenty-eight years, much longer than the time she had left. Every day that she went to work in the textile company, she carried this—the owl in a phase of flight, consuming her, stretching and adapting—with her in her mind. There, she did as she always did, cutting fabric into unwasteful, quality samples. In the windowless rear of the building, she pictured the owl as he moved through the sky about to get what he wanted, his wings muffling the turbulent air, and his frame maneuvering the forest trees. She bit into her banana.

Landfills

Landscapes. Landfills. Landholdings. Landgraves. At the time, Sylvia preferred words beginning with "land," and as her parents we did what we were told. Landlessness. "She is referring to our life," I said one morning to her father of what our daughter had inevitably overheard. That summer, the three of us deposited ourselves temporarily on my family's property in rural Oregon until we found something permanent in Salt Lake City where we would relocate for jobs with dental insurance. In other words, we took our time wrapping our heads around leaving what was home. We landed summer teaching jobs in nearby Corvallis, and the Episcopal Church had a nice daycare, which we enrolled our daughter in without a fuss. The rest of our belongings, after giving most of them away, were packed inside of our own personal family scapegoat—a shippable storage container that we'd rented and filled, and which I believed would sit on the sidewalk where it shouldn't have been until we would eventually be required to tend to it.

The house that was ours for two months in the summer was situated amid rows of crops, plush deep forests lined with wild, thorny marionberries, a regional cross-bred berry released in 1956 that left deep color stains on the skin. On the property, work began early with pruning and spraying the vines to keep them moist in Oregon's summer heat, something that had not been necessary in the past.

Mornings in the summer house were routine. I assembled breakfast, oatmeal. The one dish my father made for my brother and me growing up, which my daughter partly consumed while demanding Cheerios, only to be passed a banana. On her stool, gazing out the window at the forest, I reminded Sylvia that at least one scholar believed that oats were clever and worthwhile. Oats began their agricultural career as a weed, and survived because of their ability to mimic the global market's preferred crops of wheat and barley.

Midway through not getting anywhere with these short-circuited early morning lessons, her father would relieve me for a bit so that I could do "whatever it was that I did down there in the basement." The child and her father both agreed the basement and "whatever I did down there," was ultimately to blame for my mood, which was disrupting their lives. (An accusation left bare and without an adjective.) Her father thought that I should consider medication, but he wouldn't consider that he himself might be the one who was depressed.

There were outlines drawn on paper down there that had to do with humans and land. One such drawing was of a buffalo head and torso with the body of a semitruck—If this doesn't make sense to you, I would tell the two of them, then don't expect that anything else might. The child and her father told me to go, and that it's totally OK to take a family break. Though I'm not certain how much of this language Sylvia understood. In the basement, on the walls I'd thrown up—like a homicide detective does her crime-solving materials—were dozens of amateurish drawings, and musings on the neighboring Coffin Butte Landfill, our region's designated scapegoat, as I came to see it. The basement was also where the hefty sex books that her father and I had dutifully brought with us were stashed. There they were, piled on the cool floor. Her father and I held out hope that time itself still had prospects. But that, too—time—I had come to believe had diminished just as other resources had due to the changing climate. Though I could not yet prove it.

Not long after I was down there, cultivating a philosophy of disaster, Sylvia called out for me, and I obliged. I am her robot. Sometimes proudly, always masochistically. "Come back, Mama," Sylvia said upon my return to the kitchen, where a banana peel lay before her. I went to brush her curly hair back, away from her mouth and eyes. She needed space, she then told me, pushing me away. So, of course I followed her to the bathroom—where the razors were kept and the toilet bowl cleaner—dutifully. Sylvia generally took her poop in the morning, and as she would do this, she would ask that I remain steady on the other side of the door until instructed to come inside to watch the toilet flush. The swirl of water appealed to her. Our disappearing waste did too. In this moment, as the toiled bowl refilled, I would return to Coffin Butte Landfill, which in about an hour's time we would pass on our way into Corvallis. Humans have a need to deposit our output into some kind of vessel. Lovers, landmines, too. Progeny. Burying deep our marbled psychologies, miscalculations in judgment, our politics, in our impacted soil, our children, our subconscious, our landholdings. In the stories we start and spread. In the secrets we store. But it would and it does seep out of the body…

"MOM!" Sylvia gave me razor-eye.

She usually called me "Mama." This departure from the norm was suggestive of her intolerance to my zoning out. I told her to turn on the warm water and to use soap on her hands, while I continued talking about how we are frightened of our bodies and our animalness. This had cyclonic effects. We were origins from origins. "Landslides create landfalls that can become landforms," I said to Sylvia, who had really had enough of her mother. "Origins can be encapsulated: landmarks, words, Christmas stockings, gas tanks," I told our daughter, who by then was using the hand towel on her feet and looking for the hawk that usually hovered above the line of trees belonging to the woods.

I've read, unprofessorally, about scapegoats. In one version of the Bible, a sacrificial goat bearing the weight of humanity's sin would be sent into the wilderness, and with it, human accountability would evaporate. Scapegoats, like landlopers, heretics, or the buffalo—things with no opportunity to make their case, those things which are seen to obstruct progress—are persecuted or sent off to die. I told Sylvia that if we kept more goats around, they'd delight in eating the poison ivy, and then perhaps fewer poor people would be poisoned by weed killer; perhaps then our soil would be blessed to gain additional nutrients and humans would not need Metamucil to ease their constipation.

"We've an eye toward annihilation," I sort of kept to myself. As a social and political practice, the wild get eliminated. An entire species, such as the buffalo, or an entire geography, like two buttes in Utah, were such examples of this sort of dismantling, I also did not say. I would keep to myself my fear her asthma will worsen. The air in Utah could also be an issue. Inversions, as they were called. Though often only recorded and identified as such after the fact, after the pollution was settled. Only afterward were residents advised to carpool or to use other modes of transportation. Gas was cheap though, so the incentive was nil. And what's air?—one commenter wrote on a local television station's forum. A disaster—a petri dish of ill, trapped within glorious mountains in an otherwise uninhabited state—which I could not help but read about.

"MAMAMOM!" Sylvia yanked at my shirt.

It's time to go back to the uneaten oatmeal and her father, she said in her way of the mood in the bathroom souring. I wanted to press her to my chest like a bird has a place in its nest, but I feared getting too attached. I worried that something dreadful might happen, and quickly, like the loss of my mother.

The three of us piled into the car to commute into Corvallis, otherwise known as "town," and moved through the landscape like a cartoon. At some point we would pass Coffin Butte Landfill on our way into teaching and to daycare. An active, empirical monument to temporality, as I saw it, that had serviced the area for many years. A mountainous composite of detritus, a contractual, obliging landform that was consuming its surrounding environment like Pac-Man. Sylvia needed a snack. I handed her prunes. She wanted golden raisins.

On Coffin Butte's website, it described the landfill's maintenance.

It explained that its shape was carefully tended to every day. And that daily, the collected garbage was compacted and covered to minimize wind-blown debris and odor, as a dressmaker cares for their fabric, which had me ever interested in landscapes as they pertain to scapegoats: Could it be that the issue with civilization is that we blame everything but ourselves? I knew I was sleep-deprived.

The Center for Land Use Interpretation in Los Angeles has said that the landscape of waste was in fact a landgrab. And that garbage was the effluent of our consumption, which flowed backward through the scenery, hence the dump-defining shape that expands. I suppose that this assessment might surprise no one, so I would like to offer a thought, to think of the scenario more in terms of the weight of our bodies as they meet with the sublimity of nature. I turn to birthing a daughter; I look at art for guidance. Anselm Kiefer's landscape, *Danaë* from 2023, hues of soft browns and brassy hay-golds, a miniature dirt erection in the middle, there to denote a tomb, where inside was a figure. In this case belonging to, as the title suggested, Danaë, who was imprisoned by her father, King Acrisius of Argos, because of a prophecy that his daughter would bear a son that would kill him. For Sylvia, this could be conversation fodder over breakfast oatmeal.

"Maybe there wasn't a Golden Age," I said in the car on the way to town. Her father was busy focusing on the road, as heaving trucks passed us by on one side, and on the other, slow-moving tractors. On our commute, I explained to the air circulating in the car, I would remind my family that scapegoats can take on many shapes, like effigies. Her father had remained miffed about my messy preoccupation with blame, turned messier language arts project in the basement, where I spent time alone. He had long-term goals, you see, which included being invited back each summer to the Oregon property, and teaching at the nice university in Corvallis. There were other scapegoats in the basement, keeping the landfill company: a mapping of dead heathens spanning centuries; a list of valuable weeds either or scheduled to be eradicated; landforms. On numerous occasions, Sylvia made note of the fact that there were no goats in the basement. There was no land down there, our daughter complained. I had more to give, and so talked forward into the air that was my family, that had rightfully grown stale.

"The things that we demand carry our blame can be shapeless, like a ghost or odor; they can also be embedded, like the dump," I said, acknowledging it as we passed by.

I was in my mid-forties, maximizing my chances to reach a kind of clarity, while taking supplements for the fifty+ consumer that I began hoarding when I turned thirty, which was some time ago. I wasn't taking any chances. By the time of the dump-waving in our routine, Sylvia was screaming for her orange chew—a nutritional gummy from Trader Joe's that we gave to her to make eating count. Ever since we read in the newspaper about food's increasing lack of nutrition, we bought vitamins. I've come to have a deep appreciation for the landfill.

"First our flavor and now this?" her father had asked the day we caved and bought candy sold to us as necessarily beneficial. That day, he'd probed the drowsy teenager checking us out at Trader Joe's if she'd read about the cancer-causing colors used in snack foods targeting children. "What happened to being in the woods and *not* eating the enticing shiny red berry?" Sylvia's father asked the teenager working the register. Luckily, that week, I'd stashed a crinkled five-dollar bill in my pant pocket, which I shoveled over to the kid with a hopeful rainbow sticker on her shirt, who looked like she was about to sob.

We arrived at the daycare on the early side, so that her father and I could grab a big, iced coffee before teaching back-to-back classes. On the way to our trusty café, we found ourselves singing: "tick tock, tick tock, tick tock." "Hickory Dickory Dock" was still playing on YouTube, even without her there. Lydia Millet has written on a lot of subjects, including children—how we consciously work to wean them off nature. Children played with animals, which they later traded in for dolls and trucks. Millet writes that as a culture, we subscribe to the belief that to learn how to be human, our children must be surrounded by animal imagery. But then, culturally, we sever ourselves from the wild. We sublimate our desires to laugh loudly out of fear. We look to tidy up nature. We experience shame of our bodily functions. We determine that our underarms must smell of "sea breeze." All of that of course would come after the stuffed animals, but nothing will be spared.

These displaced sensations—which was to say our detachment from those things which were innate like ourselves—must be given a residence in an outcome, much like a depository. Like Salt Lake City. Or her breakfast of oats in the toilet bowl. Like landfills. There it was every day—a beacon of residue, the bank of our bodies in plain sight off the highway, surrounded by farmland and forest, placed on a piece of land which was and needed to be cared for like an English garden. To keep the debris down. To tame the pile of trash.

Her father and I didn't use the landfill to deposit our trash. We refused to pay the additional cost of the dump. I don't know what it was that we were trying to avoid, exactly. Adulthood? Perhaps. We did feel like we were getting away with something, pulling off a caper, but it was just trash. Nothing more. Instead, we went out of our way to dispose of our diaper-filled bags inside of the heavy blue dumpster belonging to Walmart, and tried not to be seduced into buying more things that we did not need, like purchasing additional extinct stuffed animal "lovies" to add to our colony of toys (as Lydia Millet notes of our ironies). Her father and I should have been making use of our sex books in the basement. We should have been agreeing to things, such as answering each other's questions, or that scapegoats have a long sordid history and we should avoid abusing them, too. We should just buy Cheerios, seriously. I added the item to my grocery list along with some others I was willing to try. Perhaps these things will lighten the mood.

The heat wave cruising through California eventually hit Oregon. Nothing made sense, even with an updated breakfast of a mix of

Honey Nut and Plain cereals. We took a pause on our commute. We turned to teaching online. We relocated to the cool basement where Mama's renderings of scapegoats hung on the walls, reminders of what to watch out for. The dump image was there now, next to the others. Paper squares depicting unfinished ideas—lost causes. For a time, we can subsist without water and without food. But not air, I tell my family. But the child and her father were napping. The fires in Oregon and California were raging.

By evening, Sylvia asked that I read her "best friend." A story about a black-haired kid named Moon who wore purple and learned to be free from a pack of wolves that she followed like a charm into a forest. After, our daughter wanted music. By nightfall, we'd run through every variation of "Old MacDonald" on YouTube, which we do not subscribe to, and therefore are tortured by. We felt like we were back in the pandemic, but it's of another sort. Our daughter sang out a mismatch of animal sounds: owl, cow, cat. I thought again about buying the makings to build an outhouse. Or to simply leave; perhaps disappear into the landscape, except that was not possible. (I was exhausted by these songs. I would stand out amid the trees.) But I would not leave this family because imagining what our daughter said and did next was what I lived for. Plus, no version of the song was worth it.

Day Care

She eventually wrote this about herself: *I do not deserve nature. I want to have sex in the daylight.* She would not include in her dating profile where she was raised, on the West Coast with drought-appropriate faucets and toilets, and chickens. (Her mother had kept them around for company, and for food.) She understood the potential consequences of presenting her needs completely yet concisely online. The advice, overwhelming, that she had scrolled through recommended doing the exact opposite. Females advised other females to save themselves from immediate or eventual scrutiny by hiding their true self.

Before going to all the trouble of building an online profile, which was enormously time-consuming (she had a job and an infant to care for, alone, in Los Angeles), she first ran the idea of seeking daytime sex by other mothers online, who called her a slut, which she didn't fight, though she recognized that perhaps she would be better off looking for guidance elsewhere. She then took the sex-nature conundrum—as she came to see the proposition—to her boss, a wealthy art collector, who was also kind. She explained to her boss, an actual widow herself (not a mother raising a child alone like she was), over fistfuls of fresh bread, that she had found this specific platform for weirdos on recommendation from the other mothers who had publicly slammed her for being a new mom with sick slut desires, but who had privately called her their hero for putting herself out there. Her boss wanted in, too.

As they waited for the housepainters to arrive, she and her boss took out a legal pad and began compiling their notable attributes. From there, they registered the data onto the dating app open on their computers. Her boss said that she just wanted someone to prepare her a perfect omelet after fucking, and she would provide all the ingredients to make this happen. For her own profile, she had inched open a bit more—there was her fear of nature, as she wrote, her mother (an abyss), her preference for waffles over pancakes, and of course her want of sex with either gender (both have feminine and masculine auras) between when work ended in the late afternoon, and before picking her daughter up from daycare. MartyArty immediately responded, "How old?"

The doorbell rang. Her dinging phone was ricocheting on her lap. She looked to find a flurry of texts that had come in from her mother, who wrote saying that she was at the airport in Los Angeles to see her daughter. Heavy storms were on their way. Her mother loved a good storm. Everything was happening at once. The housepainters had arrived, as her boss' small dogs barked in defense of their property. She removed the breadcrumbs from the table with her hands, and thought about how she used to be a pretty good artist. Now, she made bad mom art to care for herself. The red chip bullshit stuff. (She had a dozen videos starring her daughter using plastic dinosaurs positioned inside of their refrigerator make-believing "existence.") On her own time, she labored to convince herself that the mundane, the inappropriately, excessively lackluster—soiled diapers, pumping while Googling trash pick-up schedules—was enough to feel awake. Then her aching breasts were right there to remind her of her need for nature. She had read articles on motherhood that suggested being horny, stimulating yourself, helps with the milk flow. Though the experts didn't express themselves in those exact words. What they recommended was to scroll through images of your infant as you pumped to get the liquids flowing.

She drove to the Los Angeles International Airport to pick up her mother, as she had no other choice. "Don't move to Orem. Utah's really a desert. Remember the dead squirrel?" her mother said, fresh off her flight from Portland, Oregon, hopping into her daughter's Honda Fit. She touched her mother's knee: bare, solid, beautifully familiar. Her mother refused to wear anything other than summer clothes when visiting her daughter in California. The two of them—mother and daughter—tucked inside the Fit like sticks of gum in the humid California weather, then sped away.

A few weeks before, after several days of heavy rainfall, before her mother's visit to experience more heavy rainfall, before posting her dating profile, and before the sun had come out momentarily though not long enough to dry the land—she had found a dead, very plump, and very well-endowed squirrel. Its body was on the driveway belonging to the Modernist mansion for sale next door to her duplex. She was charmed by the totem. The squirrel, despite no longer living, had an unmistakable, masterful erection, striking like the Gothic spires adorning Paris. With a nearby palm frond that had fallen, she scooped up the squirrel and shuttled him to the top of the hill in Silver Lake, where she deposited him inside of a smooth grave that she had carved from the mud beneath an impromptu shrine assembled from a half-eaten bag of Doritos, and an empty can of *Pure* La Croix. His resting place. Not far from where she and her daughter slept. Right at the hem of the sky.

Fast-forward, and now her mother was in her car, visiting without having been invited. Her mother was the reason she hadn't left Los Angeles to join her husband in rural Utah, where he had taken a new position autonomously, without a family discussion. Her mother was the reason she had not left her well-paying job managing a wealthy woman's day-to-day affairs, as well as her art collection. Her mother was the reason she had not given up their cute one-bedroom "treehouse" to join her husband, where he had taken a coveted position with an updated job title in an educational institution (Student Operations Specialist Coordinator), apparently a dinosaur role (that even the name change would not be able to reverse), that was increasingly near-impossible to come by. He had signed a one-year lease on a rental without consulting her. He was there, and now, eagerly, impatiently, waiting for her and their six-month-old daughter to join him in Utah to begin their future. Her mother had said to her daughter that to leave her role with the wealthy art collector, who provided quality kickbacks, who was notorious for her unexpected kindness—like passing her chilled bottles of real champagne from the country of France—to leave her community to move to a place where she had none, amounted to self-harm. Her boss was rich and nice, which confused people who expected her boss to be entitled and evil. Her mother made it a habit to remind her of their maternal line. The women in their family did not leave well-paying positions, reliable domiciles, kickbacks of any kind, to follow men. Men were not solutions. Men were like piping, her mother said, verbally slapping her: things passed through them up until a point. The fix could be jeopardizing and costly. You could lose everything. Those women refused to relinquish their independence. Subsequently, all female children were taught the ways of women. They were provided with a cassette player of their own, and tapes of female rock bands such as Heart. They were provided tutorials on how to masturbate, and taught how to read. This was the way to ensure a female's longevity.

"While we don't burn our witches anymore, we do everything but," her mother said, clutching onto her seatbelt for dear life while noting a black SUV merging onto the highway, not fitting in its lane, and nearly pummeling them.

"Those giant vehicles are weapons," her mother said.

Her mother asked about the dating app, which was open on her cellphone on the car's dashboard, so that she could reply to MartyArty at some point, maybe. They were stuck in traffic.

"Here's the thing," she said to her mother—she was out of time. "Days pass carelessly."

As it was, she had a large, alarming bump next to her bellybutton. It could be a hernia. Maybe it was cancer. Her hair was falling out by the handful. Her belly sagged like a Baggu bag. And her child—all of six-months—was no longer being stored there. Daycare meant sick baby. And sick baby meant she had to skip work to care for sick baby, and entertain sick baby with bad mom art, like playing kangaroo or making shadow videos or asking the internet, "What do we really know about the microwave?" Her wealthy employer was growing impatient with empathy. The thing was, she fiddled with her online profile not only to get off during the hours she was available (limited), but also to better understand why she'd ended up in her current position—raising a child alone as her mother had done. Her online profile seeking daytime sex, as far as she saw it, had the potential to be truer to herself than she could be to herself in real life under real life pressures, because the web was infinite and her car and her one-bedroom duplex—which was to say, her reality—were not.

"Is she thriving?" her mother insisted on knowing about her granddaughter.

"Yeah, she likes school," she said to her mother about her daughter's daycare. Meanwhile, she paid attention to the car in front of her while simultaneously rejecting a deep well of feeling caused by missing her daughter so enormously, which was all encompassing and mostly debilitating. Every morning, she dropped her daughter off at daycare and then drove to her boss' house near the reservoir. (Her boss collected art but did not consider herself to be an art collector.) Her work responsibilities were wide-ranging. She did things such as checking in on international shipments, liaising with gallerists, and tracking smaller orders, like homemade, patchy linen napkins procured from Etsy. Sometimes, she had one, even two hours between getting home from work and assembling her daughter's dinner, before picking her up from daycare, where the kid made no effort to conceal her preference to stay. An evaporating bracket of time for her to have sex. Meanwhile, her husband—father of their baby—waited for them to arrive in rural Utah.

There was an unpure silence between mother and daughter. Her mother changed the radio station from news to K-EARTH's classic hits. Her mother could be hurtfully aloof. She would open her heart just enough so that you might spot softness, but the effort to go inside would require a crowbar. Her mother offered to drop her off back at work. Her mother would take the Fit, try not to lose control on the Los Angeles streets, to then pick up her granddaughter and take her to play at the recreation center playground in Silver Lake. Her mother volunteered to wash the car that was nasty with grit. Her mother embraced a good car wash. As a longtime coupon-clipper, she loved a deal. Plus, the car wash architecture and culture in Los Angeles could not be matched.

Back at work, her boss had left two hefty bags of dry cleaning in the middle of the kitchen floor next to the dog bowls, which needed to be rinsed and put away. In the parking lot outside of the dry cleaners, she looked at the weather in Orem, Utah—scorching. She looked at the real estate and wished she hadn't.

She restarted her phone, hoping to start again. She put a baby wipe on her lap and watched the water leave a wet mark on her crotch. Her phone, refreshed, was back on. She looked to it for instructions. The dry cleaner texted to say that the order was ready for pickup. In addition to art-managing, she completed these day-to-day tasks, too, running errands for her wealthy boss. But often she sat in overheating parking lots, sweating and daydreaming about cannonballs. She excused herself of this mental meandering, reasoning millions of people in corporate positions wasted time.

A mosquito had left a mark on her fleshy arm. They relished her flesh. Nobody thinks that Los Angeles has mosquitos. People go on and on about it being a desert, but mosquitos worship the city. She searched "help me," and it seemed she had broken Google. She adjusted her inquiry: "How to disrupt patterns and lifecycles?" "How to offset one's own predictability?"

"Is anyone else out there totally tired of themselves?"

Google was dead. Until it wasn't: "Work on your inner peace," was one mom's advice online, when she decided to refine her search: "How to raise a child alone when your mother raised you alone and you don't wish to turn out exactly the same and yet it looks like you are identical."

She came home from work to find her daughter and her mother playing with blocks on the floor. Her daughter didn't understand her grandmother. Sure, she was a baby, but even babies could identify what was a complicated matter. Her mother had made herself a pomegranate-lime gin fizz cocktail in a mason jar, and when she caught her daughter's glare, she said people in Los Angeles start early.

"Have you seen the nannies at the coffee shop? Now that's a study," recommended her mother. Her mother's jar of gin was frosty. Her infant's little fingers had left marks on it. Her mother asked about her day and took her smartphone away. Her mother produced an old flip phone, presenting it to her like a puppy.

"Portland is analog," her mother said.

The next day, she left early for work with her working flip phone. Her daughter was still sleeping in her crib in the bedroom. Her mother was asleep on the couch, covered in layers of sweatshirts, sprinkled with plastic dinosaurs.

"Do I not pay you enough?" Her boss was in her workout gear, eyeing the flip phone, which dangled limply in her hand. She explained to her boss that her mother had given it to her to slow down. Her mother had thoughts about the internet, speed, and female power. Her mother basically believed that smartphones were the devil, and not the desirable one that knows good booze, fine ass, and reads literature at parties.

She shared several more of her mother's theories about pleasure with her boss until her boss' eyes ran out of juice. She then returned to focusing on the swatches of wallpaper. She told her boss she had to pump because she did. Her boss then went off to her aerobics trainer, which luckily was in another part of town, which meant she could have a second breakfast with gobs of nut butters without being monitored. She found herself starving after first breakfast. Plus, she could read all the glossy magazines—like, touch them, press the pages in her hands like another hand. She could be in the presence of the beautiful and eat a lot again. When her boss came back from her workout, she carried with her a refurbished iPhone

13, already activated. Her boss had added her to the family plan.

"Traitor," her mother said later that night of her daughter's new, refurbished phone when everyone was cozily assembled in the one-bedroom duplex. Why her mother couldn't just focus on being a grandmother should have been the theme. There they were, the three of them an outline of a triangle—baby-daughter, daughter-mother, daughter-mother-grandmother—around the table, eating turkey meatballs with spaghetti dripping with red sauce. A painting, she thought. Not even a bad one.

The next day was the same: the baby was asleep in her crib, her mother was passed out on the couch. She went to work. Her boss left to work out. She ate another round of breakfast—water-based oatmeal with raisins, almond, peanut, cashew, and sunflower butters—and imagined lunchtime. During lunch breaks, she would go to her all-time favorite room in her boss' expansive domicile: the sea-green bathroom with a view of the reservoir. There, on the third floor, next to the library, she studied her packed lunch—a yellow cheese on yellow cheese sandwich, on sourdough bread—and sought inner peace. She has never once wondered why the wealthy suggest that others, like the poor, look on the bright side.

In front of her yellow-layered cheese sandwich, moist in a plastic baggy, she ate fudgy chocolate and revised her view on Mary Cassatt's mothers. With chocolate from France that she had borrowed from her boss' pantry, which she vowed that she would replace, cocooned safely in her mouth, she wondered if the painter's women, alone, save for their children, dressed in their bonnets and pastel hues, did what they did in her paintings—knit, sew, stared blanky to another time and place—so as to avoid murdering their children. Mary's women had restraint. In the bathroom, she worked to release her breasts from their amassed liquid. She wondered where the abundance of milk came from, and whether climate change was to blame for making everything go moldy faster. Her tits were ginormous. Dinosaurs were extinct and she could only partially remember why.

Her refurbished iPhone sat propped against a mandarin-lilac-scented candle that needed replacing—part of her job—on top of the toilet. She devoured insanely decadent chocolates that she would never be able to replace and scrolled through images of her daughter sleeping. She consumed photographs of her child over the past six months, a ritual to compel her breasts to give in and "let down." At any moment, the nice new phone might fall in the toilet bowl and she would be stuck searching for a bag of rice to drop it into. She would have to go to Trader Joe's. She would be forced to seek out answers: "How to tell your boss the truth about the contents of their pantry evaporating when they are beginning to mistrust you?" Inner peace would be much harder to locate once unemployed. Unemployed, and worse off, she would really have no choice but to move to Orem to join her husband.

Her tits and head swelled and ached like they had finally found each other across a crowded room. Her breasts needed to get on antidepressants. Her boss knew a guy that knew a guy that could take care of that.

Then—at long last, a notification from a potential sex match. At once, feeling utterly disgusting, like a very bad mom looking for daytime sex while her child was in daycare, the milk came pouring out like art. She capped the little plastic tubs now filled with "liquid gold," a phrase someone had shared with her when she had mistakenly called it "boob juice."

It was revealed that her mother had edited her profile. Her mother had limited the men who could contact her daughter to a one-mile radius, which her mother fully understood significantly lowered her chances for daytime sex in Los Angeles. People were scheduled. The whole idea was to cast a wide net, to have options, to make things happen with little to no effort. The whole sleep-deprived mind process was about tripling her chances at finding a match.

While her boss was working out with her personal trainer, she took her mother back to the airport and told her to fly back to

Oregon. She told her that she would mail her belongings.

"You fucking love the post," she said to her mother, dropping her at the LAX curb.

"I hope you find the sex you're looking for," her mother said, and meant it.

Parking enforcement circled her Fit. Her mother got out. They waved at each other like in a romantic comedy. A cop rapped on her window, but she was already moving—the wheels were in motion. She nodded and hit the gas. Her phone buzzed. It was her mother. "Be careful of mom slogans online," her voice projected through the car's speakers. Having been left to care for two children, her mother had a thing about abandonment and anonymity, which was to say, about being disappeared. If her mother had had the chance to go to college, she would have championed the alchemist Mary Anne Atwood, who in the 1800s wrote on hermeticism at her father's bequest. Her father went on to publish her philosophical treaty anonymously. Then, after the fact, upon reading it, he went on to buy up the remaining copies and burned them. Mary Anne had given away too many secrets about nature.

Before returning to work, she stopped at Echo Park Lake. She needed goji berries from Lassens market to refill the container in her boss' pantry, which were not yet empty. Looking ahead was good thinking—the kind of thinking her mother had hoped might save her daughter. Joggers panted around the lake. The Canadian geese—which had multiplied and claimed the park as their own—quickly ran after them. She bought a cone full of chopped mango and lime from a vendor. She sat on the hood of her car in the sun, squeezing the lime juice over her fruit, and snapped a selfie. Not a succession of selfies—because fuck that shit, what happened to art?—but one imperfect photo of herself. She uploaded it to her profile. Everything in the photo looked in order. Lately, she was experiencing incontinence. That, or she would be moving along, getting through her day, only to look down and notice a boob hanging out like a best girlfriend, or her fly unzipped and wide like a whale's mouth.

Finally, her mother was on a plane back to Portland, and she was able to retrieve past messages on her dating account, from before her mother had changed it. She decided on a man in his late twenties from Duluth, whose daytime schedule aligned with hers. An engineer, who worked at Disney in the animation department. He, too, had a small child and was desperate for sex. His wife had been afraid of him ever since their baby was born. He was hoping a promising connection might relieve him from his other attachments, like changing bike tires. He was doing his finest to adjust to the shifts within the domestic sphere—children were prisms, feelings of parental loneliness could be sharp—and to resist his need to hoard his favorite sneakers that would no doubt be discontinued.

After having sex, they looked at the ceiling in her bedroom. The overwhelming sun bounced off the white walls. Her baby's crib was next to them, and it was full of unfolded, clean laundry. The engineer had on one of those handy but clunky watches that calculated his movements. She let him check his progress because he was itching to do so. She let him trace her stretchmarks. He'd been curious about having sex with a mother of a six-month-old since his wife never let him touch her after their child was born. She and the engineer had sex again. They talked about having ear wax—so much more of it than when they were kids. They worried about their children. After, she asked him to cry like an animated baby. Like, really wail in the style of one of the cartoons that he made for Disney. Obediently, he made some unconvincing noises. Try harder, she instructed. His wails sounded totally and absolutely wrong and unconvincing.

The Disney engineer from Duluth had not given his all.

"You need to throw your torso into it, like rushing toward a need that cannot be met," she explained of infants. "You should know this."

Didn't he have a baby?

It was time for the engineer to leave. She said she was grateful for the hour or so that they were able to share in their schedules. He said she was talking in that condescending way that everyone around him did when they recounted what they were grateful for. She thanked him for the daytime sex, but she needed to get going—her child didn't spend all day in daycare. Time was a luxury, which she thoroughly understood when she found herself sitting upright, uncomfortably breastfeeding into the wee hours of the morning, when the blackout curtains didn't stand a chance against the bright California light, or even in the rain, as her child who surely could not have known better repeated "DADA" mid-suck-bite while he waited for them to join him in Utah.

That night, after cleaning up and putting her baby to bed in their single bedroom, she hid out in the bathroom. Her mother called. It was raining in Portland. She missed wearing shorts, she said over the phone. It was her mother's habit to check in when it was rainy in Portland, which was to say that she called often. The two of them made up. They became especially warm when returning to the subject of the dismantling body as it aged. About birth: giving it, receiving it. About pleasure. About feeling like yourself again, and how online, new mothers talk about getting "it back," but what did that even mean when calculating time passing? How could that mean anything other than to stick your head in an oven?

She asked her mother about her boyfriend. Her mother had a durable man in Portland who lived on her same block. She appreciated hearing about this man that was kind to her mother. Sex, it seemed to her mother, held more significance later in life, when all should be said and done. But everything was just beginning, for her and for her daughter, too. They reasoned that perhaps this was the case, because over time, women became closer to their truer selves. To knowing what did please them. On the toilet, in peace, she earnestly prayed that her daughter would sleep through the night.

When her daughter was first born, she was like a goldfish. That was how her mouth, and the hospital room felt. "Everything submerged in atmosphere," she had told the nurses who were with her in the hospital that day. Babies' eyes liked to stay tightly closed, like a clam refusing to open. Her daughter was born nearly two months early.

To reach her, to get her to open her delicate mouth, she'd had to kiss her lips. Kiss after kiss. Sure enough, like a music box, her baby sprung to life.

On the toilet, talking to her mother, her baby safe and asleep in her crib, the neighbor's sensor lights flooded through the slim rectangular window. These kept her awake at night as she tried to dream on her mattress in the living room. Lit-up like an identified convict-mom, she eyed the mold developing in the shower. There was an incoming call from her husband in Utah. She placed her mother on hold to take it.

"You ready to move?" her husband asked. No. She was not ready. Not even a hint of momentum. Even the sated, erect, dead squirrel—though all those promising things—was not ready to be limp on a driveway, of all places, outside of a Modernist mansion. Surely, the animal would have preferred the cushy mattress in the primary bedroom.

"Duck duck *goose*," she said.

"You're my best friend," he told her of his loving her for twenty years.

"Bags are packed," she told her husband.

Her and their daughter's plane tickets had been purchased. The movers had been scheduled for later that week and more rain was predicted to arrive.

Crouched on the toilet seat, she wondered if her husband's place—the one he had rented in Utah, where he sat waiting for them to join him to initiate their future together—had a bathtub. One without mold. She would be sure to purchase a gray plastic whale. The sort that fits nicely inside a porcelain tub to keep the child safe. She could bathe her baby until her skin squeaked.

Chill Local Vacation

Modern life in general was heavy, Justine and Marco agreed on this. People should be actively updating their living techniques to adapt to the now, which had, unfortunately, fatally limited the scope of our sensory experiences. We were shutting ourselves down. Fed up that morning, with her coffee in hand, Justine proposed online that capitalism was rapidly turning citizens into computers. She demanded, all the while keeping her cool, that Sacramento residents get out of their shells: "What we need is to take a chill local vacation with other fellow assholes and to learn honestly in the process," she proposed to their online community.

The plan was for people who didn't know one another to carpool to the thousand-mile stretch of Sacramento levees, built in 1850 to protect the capital against flooding, to eat and socialize as best they could.

"I don't want to die a robot, do you?" Justine wrote of learning something genuine about herself in the process of discovering others.

That afternoon, several carloads of adventurers met at Marco and Justine's place, ready for whatever. Everyone had a few minutes to introduce themselves. Many admitted that they, too, had tried attending book clubs, some had even set their Zoom backdrops to exotic locations to simulate adventure—but nothing they had attempted had closed the expanding gaps between them. After some sharing, Marco handed each person that had confirmed attendance a packed lunch, which included a veggie tea sandwich, bottle of water, and a granola bar. Everyone was assigned a car to carpool to the designated picnic spot. Once outside, Marco loaded blankets and in-case items like bug spray into the car, while Justine watched most everyone that had committed to the day's adventure just depart without a word. Save for another couple who piled into Justine and Marco's sedan.

"Chill and relaxing," Marco reminded himself, on the drive to the American River Parkway, trying not to think about those people who had absconded with the lunches; trying not to stress about the fact that Justine had willingly given out her cell number online.

"Are planes still a viable option?" Marco asked the others. He especially missed plane travel. It had made him feel like he was a part of something—a passing flaneur in the sky. But money was tight ever since he and Justine had shelled out to have the black mold festering behind their walls removed.

"There is really nothing like sitting elbow to elbow, watching a rendering of an airplane fly over the country on a little screen," Marco said.

"I've got to take this," said the older man of an incoming call.

"Sorry," offered the younger woman in the backseat sitting beside him.

The older man spoke loudly on the phone while layering on SPF, and said to the others in the car, cupping his hand to the phone's receiver, that he was ready to connect on blankets in the bright sun with strangers as long as he was protected.

Justine sat in the front seat and thought about capitalism. She wondered if she should have expanded on that tidbit further in her morning's post.

"See, the flowers are blooming." Justine noted the red poppies on the side of the road.

Marco put on the radio, an oldies station. Marco did this, since sometimes after Justine said something publicly, she often threw people off, and they hadn't made it very far along into their adventure. The day was long.

The car moved along the Sacramento streets, passing joggers and cyclists. Marco's driver's side window was down. Justine noticed his

Hawaiian button-up was unbuttoned. The hairs on his chest seemed to rise a millimeter in the golden California sun. She glanced fondly over at her husband. "I love you," she whispered, but Marco didn't hear it. For the last few years, Justine and Marco had grown more disconnected. It seemed to Justine now in the sedan, that Marco had just wanted her to read his mind to simply tell him what to do—turn off the oldies radio, Marco. She would have provided him with this if it had any chance at success.

In college, people would wait in line to ask Justine to peer into them like a microscope because she had visions that people found comforting. This routine of Justine's *seeing* went on almost religiously, turning into a kind of sadistic ritual, until she broke down. Pale and weak, her moods began shifting spontaneously. She could turn nasty and removed without approval, and this made her deeply apologetic and unsure. Those people, who originally lauded her for what she could do for them, came to despise her for letting them down. Justine became desperate for these two distinct "Justines" to resolve their differences. The gentler one that could feel emotions and offer people what they needed to hear, and the colder Justine that resented how that very effort was devouring her whole. Unresolved, she checked herself into a mental health clinic. Marco would visit her there every day, bringing her packets of oatmeal and filling her room with books.

"There is America's past informing the present," Marco said, pulling the car over to point out the California State Railroad Museum, which depicted the construction of the Transcontinental Railroad and a time of greater connectedness. The older man in the backseat chuckled like he had bronchitis, and asked mockingly if they had signed up for a tour of Sacramento. "What happened to a chill local vacation?" he asked, then went on to mumble something vulgar about tight neon biker shorts on grown men with grown male body parts, before again talking about summering in France. His second wife used to call the town's local aristocrat, who showed up to summer festivals with stories of her descendants coming from medieval luxury, rat scone face.

"Especially wicked," the older man said, "since in France they don't even eat scones."

"Are you OK?" Marco was genuinely curious if the man needed anything. "We've water," he added.

The young woman in the back pinched her thigh, hard. Justine noticed. In general, provocative displays of nastiness disguised as humor made Justine anxious. The older man was silly, and probably harmless, and she had always believed that people weren't cruel to start, right? Like, from birth. Like, straight from their mother's womb. But the internet could make them that way in nanoseconds. Humanity was full of rage. Guns were easily accessible. Justine thought about love and the young woman, and tried to picture what her life was like with the older man.

"What if we were to just ask for what we needed," suggested the young woman in the backseat.

"What do you want?" asked the older man.

"Has anyone else noticed the van that's been following us very closely for several miles," Marco wondered.

They stopped at the light that had just changed to red in Poverty Ridge, a wealthy enclave named after the capital's early history of devastating floods, before the big levees had been built to protect residents. There was wailing and honking. Some dudes in their van in the lane next to them were drilling on their horn.

"JUSTINE—you get our text or WHAT?" the dudes in the van yelled.

Justine had received it: "We need to engage in the heat vacation," followed by five rows of honeypot emojis.

The dudes in the van shouted: "We're CHILL and READY!"

"No, we hold the destination plans!" Marco responded, increasingly upset that Justine had given out her number and that he had been reduced to competing with younger men in a van.

"Do you know those invalids?" asked the older man from the backseat.

"They are my friends," the young woman explained, winking at Justine.

"Those are her friends." Justine winked back.

"Everyone was supposed to be a stranger for this to work." Marco was not happy.

The light turned green. Both vehicles sped off.

Just before reaching their local destination to relax along the levees, their sedan was rear-ended. Marco stepped out into the bright day's light to make the requisite insurance exchanges. In the backseat, the older man went to soothe the young woman. His hands swirled around her knees as he inched his way up to her thighs, for no other reason than to feel himself doing what he wanted. Justine recognized this behavior. An old boyfriend used to do the very same "calming" act with her, when it was actually the old boyfriend who was terrified of the unknown. Marco would never do such a thing.

Marco came back into the car to say they would need to wait. Justine leaned over to kiss his cheek. She passed back squat plastic bottles of water. Marco passed back small bags of complimentary peanuts, relics from United Airlines that he had pulled from the glove compartment. They were a good team. Marco suggested they read something. They might be stopped a minute. The trunk of their car was fuming; Justine noticed this and felt the makings of a larger fire. She took a magazine out from her satchel.

"This essay is about a couple's long-held ideas about themselves being demolished after traveling to Cuba in 2014," Justine assured nobody, searching for the part in the essay she was hoping to share.

Justine read: "We left Cuba and made a promise. We promised our new Cuban friends that we would never forget them or that island jewel..." Justine would not have a chance to finish before the older man in the backseat opened his car door.

"And now we'll get a Lyft," the older man said, going to leave, extending his hand to the younger woman who remained seated.

"This," she indicated that she was referring to the two of them, "is a big misunderstanding."

Back at home, Justine thought that maybe it was a good thing that nobody ended up together on a patch of wilting grass to eat the little veggie tea sandwiches that Marco had carefully assembled. The clouds were rolling in, and Justine watched them from the window in their living room as Marco prepared for them an early dinner. For centuries, painters would pass their time honoring the open horizon. Justine realized that the chill plan she had proposed for that day—in fact none of her proposals—would be able to save their marriage. Why had they fought it? Justine wondered. She watched a baby bird perched on a thin delicate branch sway in the wind. When it came to the bird, there was nothing to worry about. The bird would know what to do.

Later that night in bed, Marco joined Justine, and together they scrolled Nextdoor.com. There was news to be consumed. Pages full of updates about the piles of fecal matter that had been showing up around the neighborhood, which, when studying the photographs that had been posted, appeared to have been left by a very large and menacing animal. "A threat," many on the platform had suspected of the stinky piles. "A warning," others had said. A few important details had emerged since Justine and Marco last checked. The feces, which had been previously, erroneously, identified as belonging to a "diseased coyote," "a starving mountain lion," "a sadistic bear" were in fact the product of a human being. As it turned out, the culprit was not a deranged animal out to mangle children or endanger the neighborhood, but a pregnant woman in her third trimester, round as a hot-air balloon, who had been identified by a security camera and called upon to defend herself. The woman, close to giving birth, who lived in a less desirable neighborhood, explained to her quickly growing list of online haters that she looked forward to her daily walks on T Street, which she called "nourishing." She explained that there had been times when she could not control her bowel movements, and confessed that she went out of her way to find portable toilets—many houses in the well-to-do area were under some kind of construction—but every time she came across a temporary toilet, it would have a padlock on the door. As a result, she had found herself hiding out behind sheds, trees, and garages, tucking herself away behind recycling bins, squatting among the hedges and beneath decks to relieve herself. Before apologizing multiple times online, the pregnant woman wrote that the strangest part of the experience was how wonderful it felt to relieve herself in such a way, in the open.

"I'm not sure where, as a species, we are anymore," Marco said before turning on the ceiling fan with the remote he kept on his side of the bed.

Justine told Marco again that she loved him. She did love Marco. Marco had been a good friend as far back as college, when he would visit her in the hospital where she had gone to revive herself. He was the first to understand that she needed to hold some parts of herself back and safe in order to continue living. She was grateful, and about to share her appreciation, when she realized Marco was fast asleep.

Justine went into the kitchen for some tea. She put the water on to boil. She poured herself a glass of scotch on ice. She leafed through the magazine she was looking at earlier in the sedan, searching for the part of the text in the essay that she had wanted to share with the others about the husband and wife who had gone to Cuba in 2014. They had promised every Cuban they met that they would never forget them, but upon returning to American soil, the man and woman would forget. One day they realized it, and the truth about their self-deception rattled them to their core. They were highly educated people who should not turn into liars. They weren't the deceivers. Their condition was labeled "pre-traumatic stress syndrome," caused by the threat of what we know we know, and do nothing about.

Justine's scotch was done. The tea had steeped plenty. She rung out her tea bag. She put her empty scotch glass in the sink. She was deep into this ocean of feeling when her phone chimed on the kitchen counter, where it sat charging. A text message from a number with a Sacramento area code, which read: "It's me, from the backseat. Sorry to bug." It was the young woman from earlier.

"No bug," Justine texted back.

"Hi."

"Hi."

Something lifted, as an air humidifier softens a room. The young woman asked if Justine still read minds. The woman asked Justine if she would go on vacation or take a trip with her, even on mushrooms.

"Let's go," Justine suggested.

"I'm here, outside."

They met in Justine and Marco's totaled sedan in the driveway. They listened to white noise and made out so hard that they knew they were leaving hickeys. They caressed one another using the backs of their arms and elbows, and talked about their childhood. As a child, the young woman had wanted to be a pilot. Justine dreamed she would be a professional dancer. Now they both worked remotely. They weren't even sure what their jobs were anymore. The air cocooned around them as they made out. They fell asleep.

Justine dreamed one of those dreams which felt real, more ever-present than ever-present ever felt in her waking life. In her tangible, proximal-to-reality dream, Marco was satisfied with the decisions he had made over the course of his life. He was at the airport. His plane ticket had indicated that he was in Zone One, and so he was able to board the airplane before anyone else could. He was also able to stow his bags easily. He was satisfied. In her proximal-to-reality headspace, Justine found herself on a majestic cliff that did not spark concern. She was looking for herself down by the beach. When she found her amid the lively, sunbathing crowd, the Justine that in her youth was gifted at feeling other people without those feelings depleting her, took off her robe and wandered down the steep overgrown path to the salty Pacific waters to join herself for a swim. "I see you," she said to her. "You, I see," she said to her.

The sound of rain on the windshield awakened Justine. The young woman was no longer there beside her, and Marco was outside of the car, holding a soft blanket in his arms, asking her if she was willing to return inside where it was dry.

A Celebration

Jimmy was outside of the apartment building, ready to walk. He had brought with him packets of leblebi, a treasured Turkish snack of dried chickpeas. "Still your favorite?" Jimmy's questions would continue to deepen from there. "Is Jesse with you?" He was eager to know where my teenage son was, while Joachim's absence seemed to go unnoticed.

He passed me snacks, and insisted on knowing why I was back in Istanbul. Not only to the city, but to the European side, to Simone's apartment, in the same building, in the exact neighborhood I had lived in years ago.

"Go to Moda," he said. "The entire neighborhood smells of the sea and feels celebratory, and the quinoa is a fair price." Jimmy continued to take issue with my uninformed, therefore poor, decision to do basically the same thing I had done eleven years before. My decision was anything but basic.

"Jesse is on his way to kneel before a plaque with a letter to the future," I told Jimmy about my fifteen-year-old son, who was on his way to Iceland.

Jimmy took my hand and my heavy backpack excitedly, like a grade-school buddy. Together, we made our way through Beyoğlu cautiously, with my belongings in tow, traversing the narrow city streets beside a gridlock of yellow taxis. As we did this, Jimmy complained that while I had been away, he had grown rambunctious and horny. Three years ago, his divorce was finalized. His ex-wife had an affair with the fishmonger who owned a market on the ground level of their apartment building, and had become pregnant. Ultimately, it was she who left Jimmy. Jimmy, I suppose much to his credit, could care less about the infidelity and explained that he'd tried to make the marriage work. With noticeable difficulty, he remembered that after their separation, it was he who had tried to get ahold of her to see if she'd needed some of her books returned. And it was she who avoided his calls. He became far too interested, verging on boyish obsessiveness, in her Twitter feed, and how she described herself on social media as being happier than she'd ever been in her entire life, ever. "Her entire life," a redundancy, as he saw it. His ex-wife posted photograph after photograph of herself pregnant with the fishmonger, snorkeling and riding bareback on the Aegean Coast. All these tantalizing pictures of the two of them swimming with dolphins and jumping out of airplanes. It wasn't from her directly, but from Facebook—the most predictable of all social media platforms—that he had learned she'd moved with her newborn daughter and the fishmonger south to Bodrum, a posh Turkish city known for resorts and pristine beaches. And despite his attempts to confront her, she could not, and seemingly would not, supply the answers Jimmy needed to really move on. He said he felt invisible much of the time, barring his girlfriend, who gave him a glimpse into happiness and purpose. They had casually adopted a stray cat, who they called Unnamed, and who had to be fed. There were his university students who verified his existence. "Maybe you need to shower more or try rinsing, which is basically hassleless," I suggested to Jimmy. This noticeably rubbed him the wrong way, but Jimmy was far too eager to demonstrate a degree of maturity rather than to let me get under his skin that easily.

"Do you like cats?" He knew I was impartial toward house pets, preferring amphibians and felines in the wild.

"They've found that the parasite *T. gondii* can turn a rat's instinctive aversion to cats into an attraction by rewiring the circuits in the brain that deal with primal emotions, like anxiety and sexual arousal," he explained, resetting the course of the conversation.

I went on to say, much to his disappointment, that the way he talked about his ex-wife and their separation suggested that there was much more to the story than he was willing to share. Had he desired children? He immediately looked sheepish. Truthfully, as I said to Jimmy, in the way he had described her—his ex-wife, a woman I had known for years—I could no longer see her. It seemed to me that it was she, and not he, who was invisible in his rendering of their life. Perhaps if Jimmy could sort that out then he would be allowed to re-enter time.

"Then again, I know nothing of love," I said of my need for gratifying answers to existential yet domestic calamities.

I had left a house full of anniversary plans, a home with a perceptibly decent husband in a calm neighborhood with trees in Los Angeles, to return to Istanbul to retrace my steps to see how I had arrived at this point—a rotating spigot trying to find my position in the picture, as I saw it. My only other plan, other than examining the present in light of the past, was to celebrate: "Bigtime."

A bird took a dump on Jimmy's shoulder.

"Have you missed me?" he asked with a laugh.

Feral cats scaled the stone vertical retaining walls. Others roamed the city streets, or were at rest in their makeshift houses—cardboard boxes containing worn garments left out by the residents. The district was full of strays. There were thunderstorms in late summer; some of the domiciles made from boxes had umbrellas affixed to them, fastened above them to trees, or telephone poles, albeit broken ones since nobody could afford to do otherwise. From a distance it looked like the set of a movie for children, a collection of colorful miniature houses strung together.

We passed a bustling café on the famous pedestrian avenue, İstiklal, full of beautiful people sitting together smoking, talking excitedly. Jimmy and I sat at one of the tables farthest from the smoking. "It's one thing to poison yourself and an altogether different thing to be poisoned by the youth," Jimmy said. It was hard not to agree. I sat opposite him, facing the wall, thinking about the various ways I had poisoned myself over the years, both intentionally and inadvertently. And because he and the wall were all that I saw, I looked at him closely as he eyed the menu. I had known Jimmy for years. He was one of the first friends Joachim and I made in Istanbul when we arrived in 2014. Joachim would write and I would pay the bills by teaching English.

Close up, looking at Jimmy now at the café, he still had plenty of facial scruff, from years of refusing to own a sharp razor. His teeth were stained from drinking coffee. A necessity, he'd once explained, of being a history professor. He still wore his wedding ring. His eyes remained glued to the menu. Jimmy talked about what it was like to be lonely in a country that doesn't belong to you. That will never belong to you. Jimmy wanted to know why I hadn't said anything earlier about visiting.

The waiter returned with our drink order. I shuffled in my seat, trying to wrestle the underwear out from in between my buttocks, which is not easy to do if your goal was to go unnoticed.

"Your hair looks great, full, famous, shiny," Jimmy said.

It had grown very long and unkempt, which others had commented on being sort of like the Kardashians', minus the face and body and all that. Joachim's parents had also noted its unhelpful length and unruliness, "like a horse's mane," they said, before going on to express a deep, compulsive concern over the upcoming anniversary pictures that would be taken at the celebration, and what guests would be left thinking about our marriage.

*

On arrival back to the building, the one I had lived in before, much to Jimmy's annoyance, I collected the keys to the apartment from Erdem. Erdem, an age-defying gentleman in his mid-seventies, acted as the building's manager. He had done so since the time we met years ago. He was a fixture in the community. He was also the cute live-in boyfriend of a Canadian woman who was in the country sporadically, which was to say, when it suited her. Erdem provided keys, internet access codes, collected rental deposits, ran visitors through the building's rules, and more generally the areas do's and don'ts. He provided this service for the property's seven apartments, so that the property owners, mostly foreigners, could profit while away.

Erdem greeted me warmly and without judgment. He had scanned the contents of my mind. We shared that sort of closeness, which freed me from the burden of explaining myself. We first met eleven years ago, in 2014. I came to the city to teach English with my then-boyfriend, an aspiring novelist, Joachim, father of Jesse, who was a toddler at the time. But that was not what I was doing there now. Erdem knew that already. He gently removed the loaded backpack from my back, and my heavy shoulder bag dangling with the United Airlines tags. It was different when Erdem did it. Unlike Jimmy, who seemed to do it out of shruggy habit, Erdem wished to be helpful. There was desire there, which was missing entirely from Jimmy.

Erdem set the items down on the bench in the apartment where I would be staying. He said it was nice to see me.

"Let's get tea," he offered.

It would be impolite to simply drop me off without having a conversation.

We found ourselves around the corner from the apartment building, at a coffee shop owned by a group of twentysomethings, who, Erdem noted, hadn't left the area to go live up the Bosphorus or move abroad. The district of Beyoğlu was an active art, entertainment, and nightlife area that encompassed different neighborhoods on the European side of the city, and was more loosely known as the foreigner's ghetto. Many of the restaurants, bars, shops, and clubs I had once known in the area had since closed, though the city still had a palpable energy. Even as we arrived at the small café, life's promise was evident. Erdem had spent his childhood in that part of the city. In the past, the area was known to be welcoming and very multicultural: it had peacefully housed Jews, Armenians, Turks, and Persians, and had done so harmoniously for decades. He couldn't blame one single thing for the dissolution of that peace. He suspected, given the recent past, that what had deflated any chance at openness, what had scared new prospects away, was the city becoming a target of terrorist attacks and government ire.

The spring weather was worthy. Not too humid. Sunny with pockets of shade. The sky tucked between the tall buildings was a tangy bright blue. I was daydreaming, wanting to ask about his Canadian girlfriend—was she away permanently, was she still awful?—but I didn't.

Some patrons at the café were reading newspapers. Others were chatting, lively. The waiter came around to address our unsteady table, which had to be adjusted with small bits of cardboard so that our tulip-shaped glasses wouldn't slide around. As the waiter did this, Erdem offered his assistance, while I watched a woman, who stood out to me as a tourist, slip on a loose sidewalk stone and drop her bag of produce, which proceeded to roll quickly down the hill. The man with her ill-advisedly began to run after it, as racing yellow taxicabs and small trucks loaded with furniture zipped around the blind corners of switchbacks, narrowly avoiding the man. Erdem shrugged and lit another cigarette.

"Americans," he pointed out, "despite testing well below citizens from other countries in terms of intelligence and competence, repeatedly believe in their superior abilities."

He added, "At least for now they have money to spend."

Erdem said that, despite it all, aging had done wonders for his mind—he came to greatly admire knowing what to expect next, he said, before looking back at the man running after the produce.

About the city changing, he felt as though in an instant those foreigners coming to Turkey, searching for something, had fled immediately, in the custom of great Imperialists, once the vision had grown dark. As Imperialists do best, we did this and then took everything with us. As it stood, the national currency, the lira, was nearly worthless outside of the country. The government was doling out credit to avoid the reality. Tourism was at an all-time low. Erdem's girlfriend, whom he lived with in Sim's building, where I now lived, hadn't been back for close to a year, choosing instead to stay in her hometown of Calgary. He had stopped counting the days before he might see her again.

"But this is Turkey," he said with a sardonic smile, "and we've seen worse."

This statement served as proof that all was not lost.

Erdem looked at me and noted—cheekily, in all sincerity—that he'd tried to quit, but that sometimes certain things must remain the same to establish consistency. Didn't I like consistency? He asked me how I was, and for how long I would be staying. He asked if I needed any plants—he had cuttings and stems to share.

"Yes," I said. "Yes, I could grow plants."

*

The sublet in Istanbul, with a slight view of the sea, belonged to a French-American heiress and video performance artist, who went professionally by Simone-Deux, locally by "Sim." When Simone wasn't traveling to various biennials, she generally spent summers in Turkey and winters in Brooklyn. An odd, if not surprising arrangement, since summering in Istanbul wasn't particularly desirable and neither was wintering in Brooklyn, but she was eccentric, which made her some fans, including Joachim. Everyone who knew Simone agreed she was worth the chaos. She was born Deborah Volner, inheritor of the Tootsie Roll fortune. That much-loved American company, which owns such popular brands as Tootsie Pops, Junior Mints, and Charleston Chews. Neither Simone-Deux, Simone, nor Sim would discuss Deborah Volner or her family fortunes—she did not find the origin of her money at all worthy of conversation.

I had lived in that very apartment once before with our baby and Joachim. A temporary arrangement until we managed to get our own place in the neighborhood. The building, which was on the corner, was in Çukurcuma. A neighborhood that I had heard translated to mean "Friday gully," a reference to when Fatih Sultan Mehmed II came to the hollow for Friday prayers before conquering the city. There were many hip cafés and secondhand shops that sold anything from ox carts, to copper bowls, to textiles. Visitors flocked to the area in search of authenticity. When they felt they had discovered something, they delighted in photographing themselves in rapid succession directly in front of their discoveries.

The neighborhood was hilly like San Francisco, though nobody saw it that way. Not even when I showed them pictures. It was dense and full of attractive 19th century structures in disrepair, along with a few Byzantine ones dating back to the 1200s. Many of these had not been renovated or turned into boutique hotels, and were much like the one I would live in: beautiful, crumbling. The streets were without adequate sidewalks, crowded with car and foot traffic, and vendors selling snacks like simit or freshly popped popcorn. In the mornings, residents would pour out buckets of water onto the pavement to keep the streets cool and the dust at bay.

Had she been there to listen to me reminisce, Simone would have said, "Oh, You." Like a cat batting at a soft toy mouse on a string.

The thing about Simone, about her apartment, about being there in her personal space again, though this time alone, was that even though I had never met her in person, I believed I would be able to recognize her if I saw her in a crowd. Inside and out, was how I felt I knew her. She had been my tutor. Take this email exchange between Simone and Joachim:

Simone: *Can't this girl catch a break?*
Joachim: *I want to break you.*
Simone: *You.*
Joachim again: *YOU.*
And this, *You, You, You, You, You, You, You, You*, an arrangement of words that went on for several email threads, pages upon pages of this stacked single solitary word *you* in a desert of white space, until she eventually ended the correspondence with: *I will give myself to you.*

In what was a colossal waste of meaning and space, and language in space.

Presently dressed up in layers of Simone's Prada clothing, I was ready for anything celebratory. I looked past my reflection, abstracted in the glass of Simone's living room window. I saw out to the Bosphorus, a sliver, further still to the ferry boats beyond, which were lightly bouncing like a dotted ribbon along the nearly still waters.

*

The ride from Atatürk Airport to Simone's apartment in Çukurcuma went quickly. The taxi driver, whose name was Ashkan, and I spent our time discussing our love of cigarettes and romantic unions broken or misguided, like mine was with Joachim. I would remain in Istanbul, probably for a period of forever, I told the driver. "A very long time," Ashkan said, pointing to the gulls swarming above the sea. Ashkan nodded approvingly, and handed me a lighter and a smoke. He rolled down the windows to let in the sounds of raving seagulls and said we would need to max our volume.

Ashkan had left his first wife and children behind to pursue his passions. Passions of a varied sort: travel, song-writing, driving, and so forth. He had felt very constricted as a boy growing up in the wealthy enclave of Nişantaşı. Ridiculous, he understood, and said as much in the taxi, considering he had access to much more than his relatives. Those aunts, uncles, and cousins lived in far-off neighborhoods. Even still, he felt trapped, almost exiled from what the country was at its core: the majority were not wealthy, not secular as he was. He had grown up among a small group of the privileged, westernized elite, yet he married early, and against his parents' wishes, a pious religious woman to anchor himself. He explained of this decision that it was his attempt to bridge a gap. Despite how idiotic he saw the reasoning to be now—it was important he acknowledge that it was brave to leave comfort and familiarity behind to feel more connected. As he saw it, he was embracing what most of the population experienced.

He would eventually leave his first wife to follow his artistic inclination. He was too young at the time to really know what life was, but he ached to know and to write about it like Hemingway or Kemal or Kerouac had written of their escapades and the landscape with insight and rigor. So, he packed his bags and left.

"But you see," he went on presently, "as I ran off to pursue these dreams, I came to recognize that I needed the support of a marriage."

He didn't feel stable without a union; it was his personal threshold. While once he had thought he might live without a wife, he one day realized that he needed one, and what better than a younger wife? As far as he saw it, she would outlive him and reap the benefits. But his second wife proved to be a disaster. It turned out that she was far too young. She didn't understand his three children from his previous marriage to the pious woman. His young wife could not see how she wasn't one of them. She was, after all, not much older than his eldest son. It became apparent that she required his guidance too, his approval, his adulation, his promise of a better future, and his three children threatened this need. For example, he said in the taxi, his daughter would be on his lap and leave only momentarily to get a sip of water, only to return to find his second wife on his lap as if to replace her. It went on and on like this, he said, and he wondered if, in the end, his wife's insecurities stemmed from her feeling like a void.

"How about you? Do you ever feel placeless?" he asked. Nietzsche contended man would rather will nothingness than not, Ashkan said. He then wondered what I was doing in Istanbul: What dream was taking me back to Turkey? I talked about the liberated sense I had felt upon landing on the tarmac. The driver asked if I was a wolf.

"Like the animal?"

I thought I was a horse.

He nodded, yes.

I nodded, yes.

After we came to a consensus, he shared that he now felt foolish leaving his first wife, and their three children, because in hindsight it didn't work out with his second younger wife either. The taxi rode along at a surprisingly steady clip, passing sidewalks with packs of stray dogs moving, too. In through the windows came the salty breeze, which moved clumps of our hair around like we were dancing. Ashkan wondered again why I had returned. He lamented that the mob was in its element and "he," as in the president, continued to encourage citizens to go out onto the streets to "defend democracy."

"Doesn't this remind you of something from the 20th century?" he asked, before wondering if I was married.

*

"We are celebrating," we had told the bartender and the other patrons who were making comments about our noticeable jubilance in public, and who demanded whatever "happy drink" we were having.

Rose and I were sitting next to each other at a bar at LAX, snacking, drinking, and catching up like old friends, as we waited for news of our delayed flights, hers to her hometown of Kansas City, Missouri, to attend a medical device conference, and mine to Istanbul. Intimate conversations are possible between strangers, especially when waiting indefinitely in an airport where there's this undeniable feeling that the air quality is as bad as it gets.

The bartender, an attractive female in her early twenties, dressed in an artfully ripped Metallica tee, eyed our empty snack bowl and came around to refill it.

"Your turn: truth," insisted the bartender, who was keeping score, and who pointed to me with a pretzel: "Doubling, what are your thoughts?"

The three of us had agreed collectively that the rules of the game were eligible for revision on the spot.

Taking bobby pins one by one out of my mouth, inserting them to keep a bun-shape steady, I told them about the weird lasagna dinner with Joachim's parents. By that point, having already removed my top, sneakers, and my favorite socks, too, which hid beneath the cuff of my pants the words *Not Human*, I had to give the two of them something better. After the radio-program episode, which involved my in-laws coming over for lasagna the night before my now-delayed flight, I excused myself and went to the bathroom. Sitting on the cold rim of the tub where I felt at home, I thought about outlines and maps—points between geographical spaces, and shapes that might add up to something like letters in a word, words in a sentence.

"Too slow," my bar friends scolded me.

The timer had gone off. I had been rambling without a clear purpose and the timer was sticky, which made it hard to set in the first place.

"This is about mortality," I said. "And so forth," I added. This seemed to please them. So, I continued: Immediately, hiding out on the cold tub, I began amassing potential airline tickets. Flights that would have me leaving the next morning to Istanbul, while our teenage son Jesse was headed to Iceland's capital to regard the dead glacier Okjökull that had been reduced to a measly ice toupee atop a volcano. He was four years old in 2014 when Ok was no longer thick enough to move and declared dead. The trip was a very early high school graduation present. No longer did I have it in me to justify delaying this gift until his senior year. I could not see any benefit in waiting.

"I like that name, Jesse," Rose said, and the bartender nodded in approval, all of which relieved me as I did not want to end up naked at an airport bar, not even in Los Angeles, but I was determined to play by the rules, and my new friend, Rose, having already succeeded in getting me to remove my blouse, was making the other patrons at the airport café anxious. The bartender on the other hand, who said all she ever got by way of entertainment in this atrociously sunny place was unexpected bad weather, was overcome with delight.

Rose said that she now really appreciated a storm cloud. Rose could discern between different types: Cumulonimbus—scud, shelf, wall, and funnel clouds—and those pocket-like shapes that occasionally showed up—those were examples of clouds sinking in real time in the air, she said, sipping her soda with lime.

"Those were called mammatus, and usually appeared after the worst of a storm has passed. Perhaps the most jarring of clouds to spot in the sky," she told us.

Rose called identifying clouds her Kansas City, Missouri, trait. It was something she liked about herself. A rare treat since, as a mother, there was often little she felt confident about. It was a part of herself which more prominently stood out to her, having spent the last decade in a high desert town in Texas far from her roots, such as they were.

"Sometimes we find ourselves missing the things we let go of first," she said.

"Motherhood is hard. I've heard this from my own mother." The bartender was not impressed.

"Good thing we're a triangle," Rose commented. She then dared the bartender to lean over the bar for a kiss, which the bartender willingly obliged, making it a wet one, before returning to the subject of triangles.

"About my analyst's couch," Rose said, presently. Rose explained that she had always been an exceptional student, and saw her obligation to interact with the sought-after mind professional no differently. So, in his office, she answered the former male model turned psychologist's questions with care, deliberately. She performed well despite having grown up thinking that the beautiful, like models, were stupid, she explained of her gallant efforts to excel in his office despite his hotness. It could sometimes take her until the end of an hour's session to provide him with a single answer, such was her devotion to excelling in any situation.

I had a therapist once. He was not hot. But he did ask me whether I had ever thought about injuring myself. I remember taking him in like air into my chest, and reminding him that I was born female.

"Let's move to tea," the bartender suggested.

Rose asked the bartender who—between the two of us—she thought was more likely to succeed in getting to their destinations first. The bartender—who paused to tell us that we looked alike, like nearly identical, "You could be doppelgangers"—said the youth of today didn't think in terms of success. Instead, she told us they were more into the uncanny. Therefore, she could not say. She suggested again that we move on to hot tea. We should use the rest of our time together to see if we were related. Rose and I took the other's hands—mine clammy, hers dry—and waited to hear what the bartender would say next: "You can find out about the truth," she said.

"There's an app that will tell you."

*

Truth: when Jesse was born, I could not call him mine. I refused to claim him. Everything about that child was a mystery, and I would leave everything about that child to remain mysterious. In the hospital, the nurses kept insisting that I hold my infant son. My husband Joachim, his parents, all those present in the room that day, hovering above me, demanded that I hold my baby. Couldn't I oblige and do what they asked? Otherwise, they warned sternly, I risked our bond. I could not. When it came to Jesse, Jesse came into this world fully formed. I wanted to behold him, as he had wanted to behold the remains of a glacier. It was this exalted feeling, which had to my mind mistakenly placed me in the *unfit for motherhood* category, that for years had proved alienating. For me, taking him in as his own being, and leaving myself out of it to regard him in awe, was a celebration.

The weird lasagna dinner began when Joachim's parents heard I was making noodles from scratch. They used their spare key to let themselves inside our house to enjoy a home-cooked meal. They were outside in the backyard, making themselves at home, having beers from a cooler they had brought with them. I had gone to throw the recycling out when I saw them lounging. "Finally," my in-laws said, about my month-long pause in cooking meals. It was then that they informed me they were simply chilling before dinner. "It's ready," I told them.

Joachim was not at home. He was out at the tailors getting a suit refitted for the party that was to celebrate our anniversary. For reasons that I suspect will eventually come to me like a brain aneurysm, it was around the dinner table that Garrison Keillor's show *A Prairie Home Companion* was raised. Joachim's parents were reminiscing about the glories of the radio program's fictional setting, Lake Wobegon. My in-laws, neither of whom had ever been to the Midwest, had decided to go there one day so that they could reach in and touch Lake Wobegon with their toes, an eventual trip which had their faces alight. A bucket list experience, they said, about visiting this invented lake in Minnesota.

"Where all the women are strong, all the men are good-looking, and all the children are above average," I added, to indicate that I was familiar with the radio show.

Plates eaten, they told me to mind my own business. It was then that the truth hit me: My in-laws did not think that the place was imaginary. Or they didn't want to.

Palm fronds slapped against the glass of the windows. There had been a storm in Los Angeles, causing power outages and other disruptions. That weird lasagna night, after I had evacuated to the bathroom, where so many characters found themselves, I logged into my United Airlines app and bought plane tickets for the next morning. Vanishing would become a word that would take us places. I thought about giving birth to Jesse, and his sibling in utero who did not make it. That baby was called a "vanishing twin." She had been resorbed, incorporated into her brother, and folded back into me, her mother. Those that write about these matters of the disappeared say that the missing person is bodiless, by which I suppose they mean that the person is not in her bed like she should be, like a good girl. Jane Goodall, at four and a half, had disappeared for several hours into a henhouse to watch a hen lay eggs. She had been absent long enough to be declared missing by her mother. But Jane had been there. The entire time. Take the story of Martin Guerre. A man from lands on the French side of the Pyrenees. A man who absented himself, only to have one Martin Guerre return home seven or eight years later. His wife eventually declared him *not the man that had once gone missing*, which then, by chance (a kind of sober cosmic intervention), Martin Guerre returns, denouncing the imposter Martin Guerre.

The most familiar variety of the disappeared, save for death, is the missing person. One is declared as such after their absence is noted. In other words, when said person should have been where they were supposed to be but was not. A departure without an explanation. Someone who has left and under no circumstance has reappeared as expected. One who continues to fail to return. This truth must be explained to those that remain. Historically, sometimes a double was fashioned as a placeholder for the absent individual. In ancient Rome, this was a "person," persona, *per-sonat*—a person who is presumed to be alive, for a period, albeit is nowhere. Perhaps also for a period. Someone who cannot be located. Yet, it would fail the mind to presume such an absent person had forgone their humanness. It seemed convoluted to me then, hiding out from my in-laws in my bathroom, planning my escape from my life, that the pain we suffer could in some cases be the result of a great misunderstanding unless there is something else? But how can we know if we are not seeking to learn?

As for me in Turkey, I would arrive just in time to miss the celebratory feast day of St. George, when the path to the monastery on the largest of Turkey's Princes' Islands, Büyükada, gets flooded with pilgrims ascending to the peak of the mountain to pay homage. The site attracted Muslims forbidden to worship idols, yet, like others with them, they came wishing for cures for illnesses or for love spells, because believing is necessary. These faithful, of all kinds, some on their knees, hiked up the treacherously steep hill, unspooling cotton yarn and hanging votive ribbons along the way.

Acknowledgements

Two Dollar Radio, we should be a basketball team. Eric, Eliza, and the little potted plants in your yard that must be schlepped to HQ on weekends to give away to the community—Thank You for nourishing things and then letting them go. Brett! You stuck around. Love you, Buddy. Dan and Ruth, Seven Stories Press, thank you pages and pages of all different shapes for your support.

Readers, Thank You:

Ashley Farmer
Amelia Schonbek
Daniel Gumbiner
Ashley Gallagher
Cressida Leyshon
Benjamin Samuel
Kerrie Kvashay-Boyle
Shya Scanlon
Lauren Spohre
Martha Wydysh
Jensen Beach
John Edgar Wideman
Erin McReynolds
Brian Conn
Elizabeth Ellen
Gabriel Blackwell
Jeff Johnson
Carolina Ebeid
Andrew Farkas
Carolina Ebeid

My friends, you cannot be matched. My family, long roads with full skies. I owe so much to you all, like my life! I love you.

NORA LANGE's debut novel *Us Fools* was awarded the The Sue Kaufman Prize for First Fiction, was a finalist for the National Book Critics Circle Award in Fiction, named a best book of 2024 by *The Boston Globe* and NPR, a *Los Angeles Times* bestseller, and a *New York Times* Editors' Choice pick. Her writing has appeared in *The New Yorker*, *Granta*, *The Believer*, *BOMB*, *Hazlitt*, and elsewhere. She has received fellowships from Brown University and is a fellow at USC's Los Angeles Institute of the Humanities. She now lives in Utah with her family.